Content

D1585629

1	It's Oh So Quiet	1
2	Growing, Growing, Gone!	24
3	Science You Asked ...	39
4	Can Dennis Dig It?	52
5	What's Tomato With You?	63
6	The Blame Game	74
7	With Cousins Like Minnie, Who Needs Enemies?	89
8	The Veg Who Lived	98
9	It'll All Work Out In The Blend ... Right?	109
10	The Widl Problem!	128
11	Souper Troopers!	144
12	Oh. My. Greenfingers!	159
13	The Vegetable Plot Thickens	168
14	Give Peas A Chance!	175
15	Bring Out The Bugs!	187
	Manual Of Mischief	203

Welcome to... BEANOTOWN!

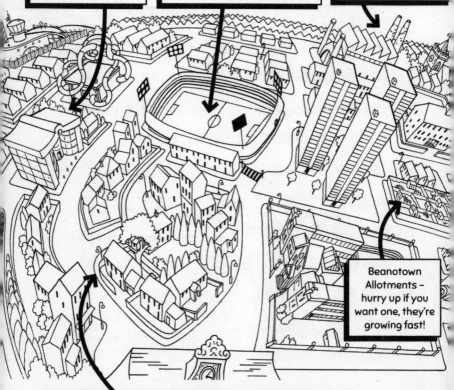

Beanotown Library, Beanotown's tallest building. It has the most stories, you see!

Cold Trafford, home of Beanotown Untied Football Club – it was supposed to be Beanotown United, but their speeling wuzn't verry goood!

Perkins' Paperclip Factory – the workers are all very attached to their work!

Beanotown Allotments – hurry up if you want one, they're growing fast!

This is where the Menace family lives. Menaces by name, Menaces by nature. At least that's what the neighbours say!

Chapter One

IT'S OH SO QUIET

April Fool's Day is also Beanotown Unofficial Memorial Day (B.U.M. Day), when the town honours pranksters of the past who are sadly no longer pranking.

Nothing *bad* happened to them. They just grew up and lost their sense of humour.

Actually, that is pretty bad, when you think about it. **SNIFF!**

> Pull yourself together and get on with the story! – The Ed.

Dennis Menace knew that **HE** was never **EVER** going to lose his sense of humour or grow up. He wanted to be a ten-year-old

prankster genius forever, and no one was
going to stop him!

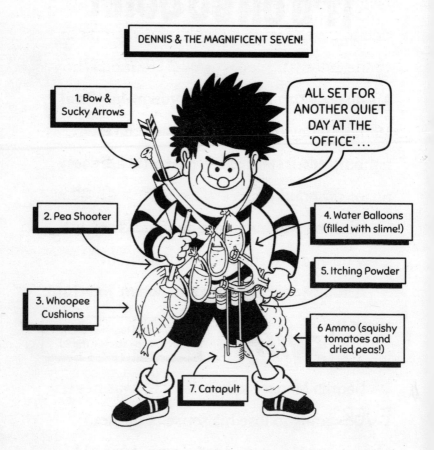

DENNIS & THE MAGNIFICENT SEVEN!

1. Bow & Sucky Arrows

ALL SET FOR ANOTHER QUIET DAY AT THE 'OFFICE' . . .

2. Pea Shooter

4. Water Balloons (filled with slime!)

5. Itching Powder

3. Whoopee Cushions

6 Ammo (squishy tomatoes and dried peas!)

7. Catapult

It was only half nine in the morning and he'd already put a whoopee cushion on every bench in Beanotown Park; hidden a fake dog poo in the museum; and glued a water pistol to the automatic doors at Widl (Beanotown's biggest supermarket) so everyone who went into the shop got squirted at waist level.

It should have been the Greatest Official Single-Handed April Fool's Laugh Of All Time Ever Recorded (G.O.S.H. A. F.L.O.A.T.E.R.), but it wasn't.

It wasn't, because none of Dennis's friends were around to laugh at his pranks.

There was no one to hear the 21-fart salute in the park.

There was no one to see Vicar Whicker faint in the museum's fossil section.

And it was almost criminal that there was no one to laugh at the shoppers who looked like they'd wet themselves.

A wise woman once asked: 'If a tree falls in a forest and no one is around to hear it, does it make a sound?'

Well, what if a whoopee cushion parps in the park and there is no one to laugh at it? Does that count as **silent but deadly?**

Don't worry – Dennis's pals hadn't all suddenly grown up and lost their sense of humour, but it was almost as bad. They had all been bitten by **the gardening bug** and were always down at Beanotown's allotments growing flowers, fruit and vegetables.

There was even a rumour that

HMM...THE SWEET SMELL OF MANURE!

The gardening bug, viewed under a microscope

someone was growing sprouts. Dennis knew that wasn't true because sprouts are actually toxic green poos that fall from the butts of intergalactic space donkeys.

Dennis had a theory that it wasn't a meteorite that hit Earth 65 million years ago and wiped out the dinosaurs. He reckoned it was a massive smelly green alien, and humans would be next to experience ex-stink-tion if they didn't stop eating its poo . . . er, sprouts.

Gnasher, Dennis's unstoppably awesome dog, loved sprouts, but he's also fond of eating

Sprouts are almost a treat, if you've tasted Dad's feet!

Dad's slippers, so he had little to fear from
a teeny-weeny-greeny space poo.

Rubi Von Screwtop was using all her
scientific know-how to measure, prune, feed
and irrigate her vegetables.

Pie Face was growing loads of stuff –
basically anything he could cram into
a pie.

Vito's allotment was 100% organic. Vito
is an eco-warrior, and an eco-*worrier*, and she
thinks organic growing is one way to help
save the planet. She cares A LOT about saving
the planet.

Stevie Starr was more interested in making
time-lapse videos of his plants growing. He
loves making his own videos and uploading
them to his You-Hoo channel.

Minnie the Minx was just growing stuff
she could throw at people.

Dennis had tried gardening, but there
was a lot of waiting around. Naturally enough,

8

he'd had an awesome idea to make it a lot more fun for everyone.

He'd gone round to see Felicity Longface-Plante, the very posh owner of *Dobbinhams*

Riding School and Stables. She'd agreed he could have as much fresh horse manure as he could get in a taxi.

Dennis set up a huge catapult and fired the manure all over the allotments. Then he waited for his victims to retaliate. The Manure Wars had begun!

Only, no one launched any manure back.
Instead, they'd put it on their crops to make
them grow better. People actually liked being
a victim of Dennis's prank!

It was the last straw. Dennis left the
allotments and hadn't gone back.

Years ago, Beanotown had lots of
allotments. Then Mayor Wilbur Brown had
closed them down and opened a scrapyard
instead. He figured he could make more
money that way.

Then, at the beginning of this year, he'd
announced he was scrapping the scrapyard
and using the site to open allotments. No one
knew why, and no one really cared. Beanotown
was growing again!

In actual fact, Wilbur had recently

discovered *Blooming Britain*, a competition to find the town whose citizens grew the best flowers, fruit and vegetables. It had been won by Chipping Compost in the Cotswolds for the last three years.

Wilbur didn't care about flowers or vegetables, but he'd been tipped off by an old school chum that the mayor of the town that won *Blooming Britain* would almost definitely win *Mayor of the Year*.

MAYOR BROWN'S SWEETEST DREAM!

MAYOR

Beanotown's worst night-mayor!

And boy, did Wilbur care about that!

When Dennis and Gnasher arrived, the allotments were a hive of activity and noise. Phones blared out Radio Beanotown, and spades were thunking into the soil in time to the beat. Or in time to the beetroot.

A wheelbarrow squeaked as Calamity James carted a load of fresh manure to his plot. Then James himself squeaked as he hit a rock and fell head-first into his pongy cargo. Poor James!

GROAN!
AT LEAST IT WAS
A SOFT LANDING!

BEST MANURE WITH FREE PONG

'Calamity' James Clover is the unluckiest boy in the world. He's so unlucky that doctors have been studying him ever since he'd had an infamous accident when he was four years old.

A piano fell on his head.

In the middle of a field.

When the paramedics arrived, they had to use a crane to lift the piano off him.

Then the crane broke, dropping the piano on poor James again.

When they finally got James out from under the piano, a kindly cow tried to comfort him, by giving him a little pat on the head.

I SUPPOSE I'M LUCKY IT WASN'T AN ELEPHANT!

Dennis walked through the allotments to where his friends' plots were.

Rubi was measuring fertiliser to the millionth of a millilitre.

'Don't breathe,' she said. 'The atoms in your breath might ruin everything!'

Pie Face was planting rhubarb, which he then broke an egg over and 'watered' it with milk.

'I'm trying to grow rhubarb and custard tart,' he explained.

Stevie was filming some ants who were eating his asparagus. He had a camera lens as long as an elephant's trunk to zoom right in on them.

DON'T LAUGH! WITH THIS LENS YOU CAN EVEN TELL WHAT KIND OF TRAINERS THEY'RE WEARING!

Minnie was draining rubber sap from her huge rubber tree to make extra-strong catapult elastic.

Vito was hammering in signs that told the bees exactly where to fly next to get more lovely nectar and pollinate her plants.

Suddenly, a loud bell rang. Everyone dropped their tools and walked to the far side of the allotments.

'Where are you going?' Dennis asked Ralf, the Bash Street School janitor. Ralf was renowned for his remarkable raspberries. The eating kind, not the funny, noisy kind.

'The mayor's making a Public Announcement Regarding Plots,' said Ralf. 'Come on, we don't want to miss a P.A.R.P. from the mayor!'

Dennis exchanged doubtful glances with Gnasher. Dennis thought he wouldn't mind missing a mayoral P.A.R.P., but he shrugged and followed Ralf anyway.

The mayor was standing on an upturned apple box. He liked to look down on people. His son, Walter, stood beside him. Walter was Dennis's sworn rival, always trying to get him into trouble.

The audience doesn't have 'crate' expectations for this long-winded lecture...

GATHER ROUND, EVERYONE! COME ALONG!

Walter's posing like he's POOP (Proud Of Our Plots)

'Loyal and grateful citizens of Beanotown,' Wilbur began, when he had gained everyone's attention.

The crowd turned to look behind them to see who he was talking to. None of them felt very loyal or grateful to Wilbur, who was usually a pain the neck and only interested in making himself richer.

'To celebrate my totally unselfish reopening of these allotments, I've signed Beanotown up for the *Blooming Britain* competition. And, to make sure we win, I am offering a massive cash prize to the person who grows the finest, biggest, tastiest vegetable. Poster, unveil the Walter! I mean . . . Walter, unveil the poster!'

> I HAVE A MAKEMENT TO ANNOUNCE . . . ER . . . AN ANNOUNCEMENT TO MAKE.

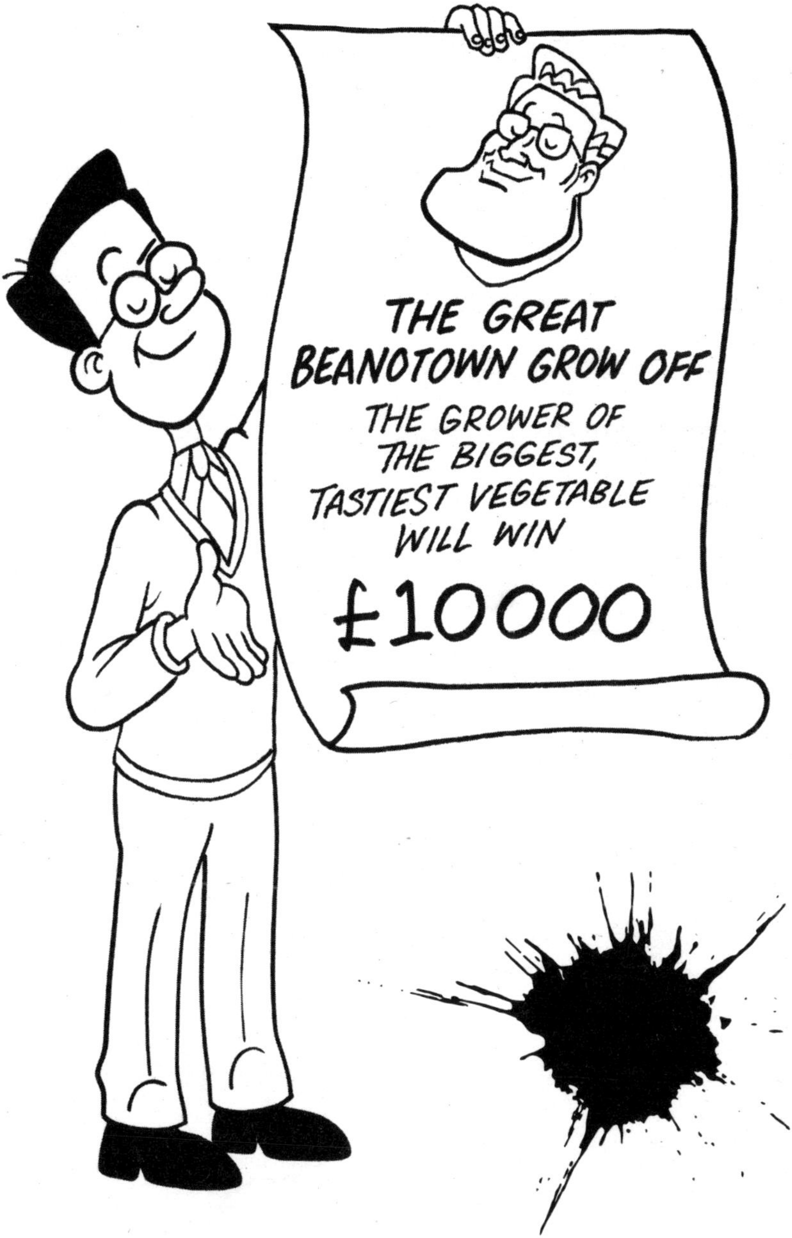
THE GREAT
BEANOTOWN GROW OFF
THE GROWER OF
THE BIGGEST,
TASTIEST VEGETABLE
WILL WIN
£10000

The crowd gasped. Ten thousand pounds? That was amazing!

Wilbur beamed. He knew this competition would get everyone fired up!

Walter had done well. He'd chosen a photograph that made his father look important, and a NICE BIG FONT for that cash prize of . . . hang on, ten thousand pounds?! Wilbur began to panic inside.

'Walter!' he hissed. 'The prize was a *hundred* pounds! Not TEN THOUSAND!'

'B-b-but I just copied what you scribbled on that piece of toilet paper!' Walter stammered. He fished a crumpled blot of toilet paper out of his pocket and showed it to his father. 'Look!'

£100.00

Wilbur took a deep breath and composed himself. 'It's my fault,' he said.

Walter relaxed.

Walter drooped. He'd worked hard on the poster and was actually quite proud of it.

'It's not a complete disaster,' said Wilbur, stroking his chin. 'You can fix this. You have to win the contest. Then I won't have to pay out to the winner.'

'I don't know anything about gardening!'
Walter would have said, if he didn't feel so
guilty. Instead, he just nodded miserably.

'Oh boy!' whooped Dennis. 'Ten thousand
smackeroonies, Gnasher!'

Gnasher yawned. He wouldn't get out of
bed for a million smackeroonies. One single
sausage, on the other hand . . .

'We've got to win that contest,'
said Dennis, thinking hard. 'It
shouldn't be too difficult.'

'I mean, I'm a borderline genius,'
he added modestly, 'and there
MUST be a quicker way to grow
fabulous fruit and vast vegetables
than all this digging
and hard work, right?'

IT'S TIME I PUT THE DEN INTO GARDENING!

OH BOY! HERE WE GO AGAIN!

Ralf the janitor was passing by.

'Nice to see you back here, Dennis. Maybe I can help you get started again.'

Dennis grinned. He was back in the gardening game!

Ralf gave Dennis some little plants in pots, and some seeds he had left over.

'Here you go, lad,' said Ralf. 'Work hard and have fun. Don't thank me – just give me your biggest cauliflower at the end of the season.'

'You bet!' said Dennis.

Ralf walked back to his plot.

'Gnasher,' asked Dennis.

'What's a cauliflower?'

A collie flower?

Chapter Two

GROWING, GROWING, GONE!

Dennis didn't really care what a cauliflower was. He knew what ten thousand pounds was and that's what made him do something he would never EVER normally do unless someone made him – he tidied up.

HANG ON!

DENNIS TIDY UP?

Yes! Dennis started to out the old greenhouse on his plot, shoving old flowerpots, garden tools and junk into the corner. He even found an old Beano comic!

'The Beano No.1?' Dennis read aloud. He flicked through the pages. 'This thing is ancient – and I'm not even in it!'

Dennis dropped the comic into the bin. 'No time for reading just now – I've got ten thousand pounds to win!'

'Gnash-gnash-gnash-gnash gnash!'* said Gnasher anxiously.

When the greenhouse was a bit tidier, Dennis started to dig. With a rake. He didn't know a lot about gardening.

*GNASHER'S RIGHT – THAT COMIC IS SUPER-RARE AND WORTH AT LEAST £25,000!

Luckily, Gnasher is a lean, mean digging machine. He put his nose into the ground and his chompers to work.

While his dog dug, Dennis followed, planting his seedlings, and then the seeds.

Soon everything was in the ground.

'I think we have to water them now,' said Dennis.

Gnasher lifted a hind leg and looked at Dennis. **'Gnuh?'**

'Sorry, Gnash!' laughed Dennis. 'I think we have to use actual water!'

Gnasher trotted outside to water the many weeds instead.

Now that Dennis had planted all his prize-winning . . . er . . . things . . . he stared at them. Nothing happened. Two minutes passed. Still nothing.

'Rubi!' Dennis called over the fence. Rubi looked up from her fertilisation chart.

'Hi Dennis!' she grinned. 'How's the growin' goin'?'

'Not well,' said Dennis. 'I planted everything at least five minutes ago and nothing's happened. I think they're faulty. Or maybe they need an upgrade.'

'It takes a bit longer for stuff to grow,'

Rubi laughed. 'You probably won't notice anything happening for a couple of weeks and

WEEKS? MONTHS?!

it will be two or three months before you can pick anything.'

'Nah,' said Dennis. 'Not *my* plants. I don't have time for that. The competition closes soon!'

'Suit yourself,' Rubi shrugged. 'If you discover the secret of growing stuff instantly, let me know!'

Dennis was worried. Rubi usually knew about stuff, and she didn't seem to think Dennis had any chance of growing a massive marrow in the next hour or two.

He went to speak to Pie Face, who was

gently stroking the leaves of a cabbage.

'What are you doing?' asked Dennis, puzzled.

'Ralf told me I had to give my plants lots of
care and attention, so I'm giving my cabbage
a massage.'

WILL THAT MAKE IT
GROW FASTER?

I DON'T KNOW, BUT I'M
HOPING IT WILL MAKE IT
MORE DELICIOUS IN A PIE.

'How long will it take?' Dennis asked.

'About an hour,' said Pie Face.

Dennis felt excited.

'You can grow a cabbage in an hour?' said Dennis excitedly.

'No, silly,' said Pie Face. 'That's how long it will take to bake the pie. The cabbage will take weeks to grow!'

Suddenly, they heard shouting from the far side of the allotments. They ran over to see what was happening. Butch Butcher and Sergeant Slipper were arguing at a water butt.

While they were arguing, Mrs Creecher sneakily snaffled the last few drops in her watering can and ran off, chuckling.

'Now look what you've done! How am I going to win that money now?' moaned Slipper.

'If it was anyone's fault, it was yours,' retorted Butch. 'I needed one for the money . . . er, for the artichokes!'

It's not like Sergeant Slipper or Butch Butcher to argue, thought Dennis. *Or Mrs Creecher to be sneaky, for that matter!*

'This is what happens when there's a lot of money at stake,' said Pie Face. 'People get grumpy and mean. Why can't they just do it for the fun?'

Pie Face was right. Something had changed at the allotments. Even Dennis could feel it.

Before the mayor had announced his competition, everyone had been smiling and helpful. There had been jokes and laughter. It was *fun* being at the allotments.

Now, people were watching their neighbours suspiciously, as if they might steal their strawberries or pinch their peas.

The fun had gone out of the allotments.

Then the sabotage began.

Dudley Jubbly's squash was squashed, Prudence Perkins' potatoes were pummelled, someone had gorged on Mr Dawson's gourds and Mr Chambers' chard had been charred.

Rubi thought she knew who was behind it.

'Fifteen minutes ago, Walter was looking worried,' she said, 'but look at him now.'

She was right. Walter was walking around like he owned the allotments, making notes in a little notebook and ticking things off.

'You think he's sabotaging other people's crops?' gasped Pie Face.

'I wouldn't put it past him,' said Dennis. 'We should get back and make sure our plots are okay.'

Rubi's plants were all fine. She'd installed an intruder-detection system anyway.
Pie Face's were safe and sound too.

But Dennis's seedlings were gone! Only they weren't *gone* gone, it was more like they'd been eaten!

'Would Walter eat my plants?' he wondered. That seemed a bit odd, even for Walter.

'This wasn't Walter,' said Rubi. 'Look!'

She pointed to the pile of rubbish in the corner of the greenhouse. From beneath it, hundreds of tiny little eyes glared out at

Dennis. He lifted the rubbish, revealing . . .

... BILLIONS OF BUGS!

'There's your plant-eaters!' said Rubi.
'Those insects have had a lovely feast while
you were away!'

'You should build them a new home so
they'll move out of your greenhouse,' said
Pie Face.

They scooped up loads of grass, twigs, leaves and bark and stuffed it into an old wooden box. Then they lifted the box out of the greenhouse and placed it in the far corner of the plot.

Dennis scribbled on a scrap piece of wood and laid it on top.

'They'll be happy in there,' said Pie Face. 'But what about your plants?'

'I planted some seeds as well,' said Dennis. 'They're still under the surface. I guess they're my only hope now.'

Pie Face and Rubi went back to their plots.

Dennis stared at his chewed-up seedlings and sighed.

> WHAT I NEED IS A SECRET WEAPON. IT'S ONLY FAIR – IT'S NOT MY FAULT I STARTED SO LATE AFTER EVERYONE ELSE. WELL, IT IS MY FAULT, I SUPPOSE. BUT WHO WOULD BE ABLE TO HELP ME?

Ralf? Nah. He'd already helped and Dennis didn't want him to know he'd killed off those seedlings already.

Miss Mistry? She grows all her own veg . . . Nah. That would be too much like being at school.

What about Boris and his family, the

mysterious inhabitants of No. 13 Frightsville

Place? They have lots of cool plants growing

at their house . . .

THIS IS VLAD THE VENUS MAN-TRAP. HE LOVES TO HAVE PEOPLE ROUND FOR DINNER.

FEED ME!

Shudder! Definitely another NAH!

'Got it!' said Dennis out loud, snapping

his fingers.

'Come on, Gnasher,' he said. 'Let's go visit

Professor Von Screwtop at the Top Secret

Research Station!'

Chapter Three

SCIENCE YOU ASKED...

Beanotown's Top Secret Research Station is a quick five-minute run for a fit ten-year-old boy and his dog, so it wasn't long before Dennis and Gnasher were ringing Professor Von Screwtop's doorbell. A Top Secret Research Station needs to have a pretty awesome doorbell, and this one certainly was!

Dennis pressed the button and a familiar tune rang out.

SOMEBODY'S KNOCKIN' AT THE DOOR, SOMEBODY'S RINGIN' THE BELL

Gnash-gnash, gnashy gnash-gnash, gnash-gnash-gnaaaaash!

The door opened. 'Hello, dancing boy and musically talented dog,' said the professor.

Professor Von Screwtop is Beanotown's top scientist and, more importantly, Rubi's dad. The professor is the most and least clever person that Dennis has ever met. He can tell you why the sun is sometimes yellow and sometimes orange, but he can't even tie his own shoelaces.

The prof has four degrees (Quantum Physics, Advanced Chemistry, IT and Awesome Space Facts), three PhDs (Maths, Physics and Super-Hard Chemistry) and a bronze Beanotown-on-Sea Swimming Gala medal.

He speaks 22 languages, one of which has no other speakers in the entire world, so sometimes he has to talk to himself just to keep the language alive. Luckily, Rubi is learning to speak it too.

He's very proud of his Top Secret Research Station and it's now the finest 'place where scientists do cool stuff' in the world . . .

BEANOTOWN'S TOP SECRET RESEARCH STATION

SPACE ROCKET GARAGE

EXTRA TERRESTRIAL COMMUNICATION CENTRE

NOISY DOORBELL

MILK FOR PROF'S EARL GREY TEA

AREA 50·5

ZOMBIE-RESISTANT BARRIER

P.E. (PROFESSOR'S EXERCISE) GYM

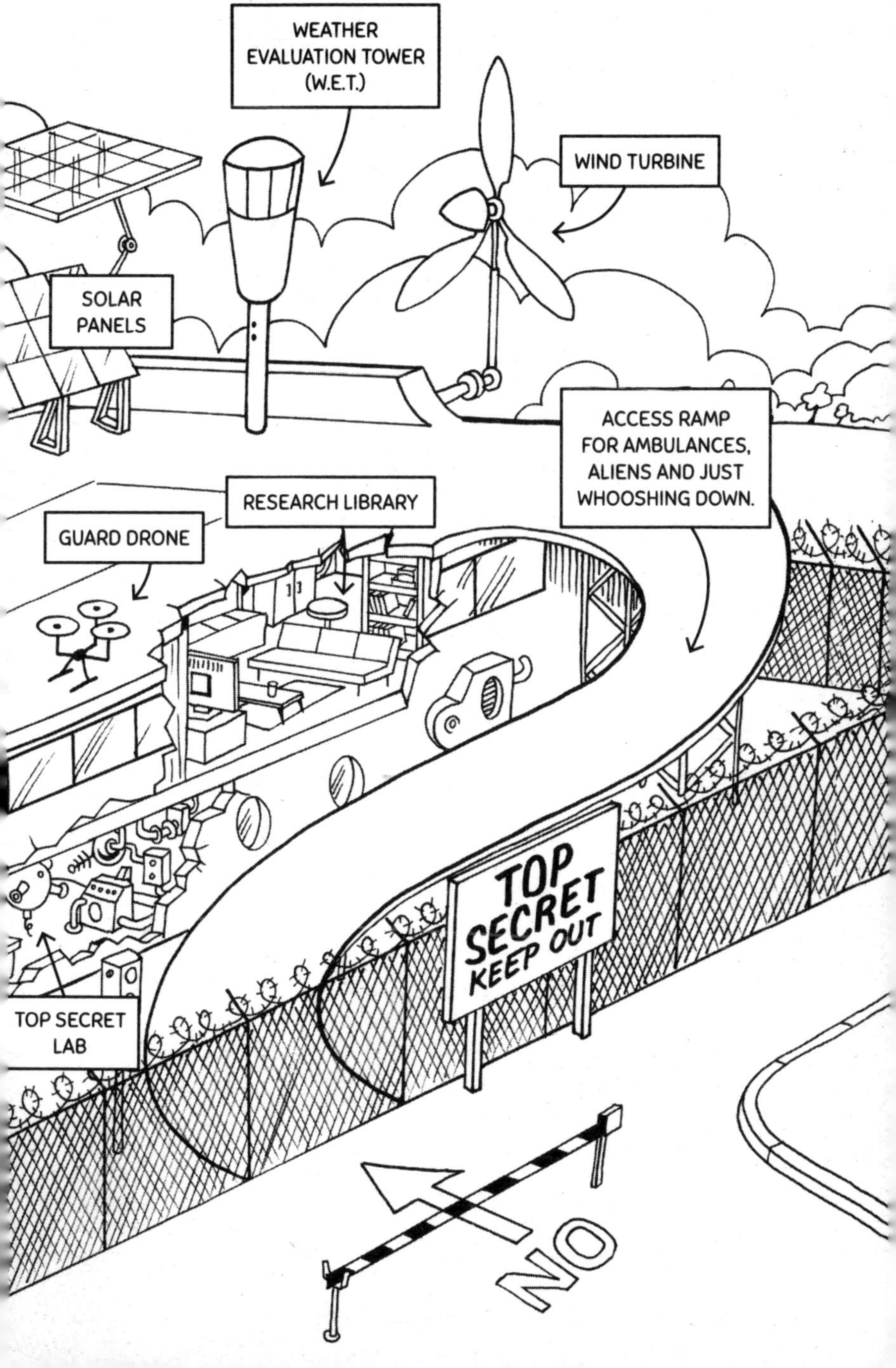
WEATHER EVALUATION TOWER (W.E.T.)
WIND TURBINE
SOLAR PANELS
ACCESS RAMP FOR AMBULANCES, ALIENS AND JUST WHOOSHING DOWN.
RESEARCH LIBRARY
GUARD DRONE
TOP SECRET LAB
TOP SECRET KEEP OUT
NO

'Hi Professor,' said Dennis. 'I wonder if you can help me grow fruit and veg faster?'

'Well,' said the prof. 'The first thing you need is a greenhouse or a polytunnel.'

'I've got that,' said Dennis.

'Next, you need to water regularly,' he added. 'But not doggy-watering, ha ha!'

Gnasher sighed. No one wanted him to pee on anything ever again, it seemed.

Professor Von Screwtop leaned closer. 'My top secret tip for growing fruit and veg is . . .'

'Yes?' asked Dennis eagerly.

'Talk to the plants.'

'Okaaaay,' said Dennis, 'what if I told them jokes? Would that help?'

'Only,' said the professor, 'if you want to grow tickled onions! **Hee-hee!**'

DENNIS'S UN-BEET-ABLY CORNY VEG JOKES!

WHAT KIND OF TABLE CAN YOU EAT? A VEGETABLE!

WHAT WAS THE SNOWMAN DOING IN THE CARROT PATCH? PICKING HIS NOSE!

WHY IS LETTUCE THE KINDEST VEGETABLE? BECAUSE IT'S GOT HEART.

WHY IS IT IMPOSSIBLE TO GET ANGRY WITH A YAM? BECAUSE THEY'RE SUCH SWEET POTATOES.

WHAT IS LONG, GREEN AND SLOWLY TURNS RED? A CUCUMBER HOLDING ITS BREATH.

WHICH VEGETABLE LOVES ROLLER COASTERS? CELERWEEEEEEEEEEEEE.

WHY DID THE TOMATO BLUSH? BECAUSE IT SAW THE SALAD DRESSING.

WHAT IS AN ELEPHANT'S FAVOURITE VEGETABLE? SQUASH.

WHAT IS A LIBRARIAN'S FAVOURITE VEGETABLE? QUIET PEAS.

WHAT IS THE STRONGEST VEGETABLE? A MUSCLE SPROUT.

WHAT DO YOU CALL A RETIRED VEGETABLE? A HAS-BEAN.

HOW DID THE GARDENER MEND HIS JEANS? WITH A VEGETABLE PATCH.

WHY DID THE CORN STALK GET ANGRY WITH THE FARMER? HE KEPT PULLING HER EARS.

WHAT DO VEGETABLES WANT MORE THAN ANYTHING IN THE WHOLE WORLD? PEAS ON EARTH.

WHAT KIND OF VEGETABLE HURTS? SPIN-OUCH.

'Isn't there anything *faster* I could do?' he asked. 'I need these veg to grow really quickly!'

Professor Von Screwtop stroked his bushy grey moustache.

'Well, I did some work on super-growth serums a long time ago,' he said. 'To speed up food production, you understand?'

'My first experiment made the veg grow and grow and grow. Even after it was picked, cooked and – gulp! – eaten! That could have ended very nastily!'

'Perfect!' said Dennis.

NOTHING A BURP CAN'T FIX... HOPEFULLY!

URM, I'M FEELING RATHER FULLISH...

'My second attempt was a little different,' the prof continued. 'I injected my vegetable seeds with dolphin DNA then watered the plants only with salt water.'

'What happened?' asked Dennis.

'Well, the veg did grow bigger but they were also very clever. They were grand masters at chess inside three weeks and eventually they figured out that if they ate all the other vegetables, they could take over the greenhouse! Those veg were clever, and ruthless!'

The professor shuddered.

YOU LOOK AS COOL AS A CUCUMBER.

I'M AN AUBERGENIUS, MATE. OR SHOULD I SAY CHECK MATE?!

'For my last experiment in super-growth serums, I thought I had better try a more stupid animal. I thought about using cow DNA, but cows turned out to be very clever animals. They love to complete the crosswords in the *moo*spaper.'

Dennis couldn't tell if the professor was making a joke or if he was serious.

'I knew that dinosaurs had teeny-tiny brains even though they had enormous bodies, so I called my friend at Beanotown Museum to see if he could sort me out with some dinosaur DNA. Unfortunately, he couldn't help, so I had to order it on WeeBay.'

Dennis's eyes were wide. 'What happened?'

'Nothing,' said the prof. 'Absolutely nothing. There must have been something that

I'd missed – the magic ingredient that would have made it work.'

Dennis slumped back in his seat.

'Groan! What is science even for, if it isn't to invent crazy dangerous mutant plants using dinosaur DNA?!'

'Well, one day I'll look into it again,' said the prof. 'Until that day, those three failed experiments will sit safely on that shelf by the door.'

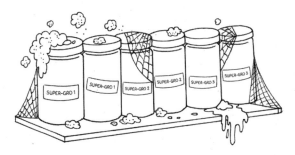

'Now, is there anything else I can help you with?' the professor asked.

Dennis couldn't take his eyes off the dusty jars on the shelf.

Then . . .

There was no dolphin. It had all been a distraction (that's a trick to make someone look away from what you're doing, not a different kind of super-smart swimming mammal). When the professor turned back, Dennis and Gnasher were gone.

And so were three jars of the professor's failed super-growth serums.

Chapter Four

CAN DENNIS DIG IT?

On his way back to the allotment, Dennis wondered which of the growth serums to try first on his newly planted seeds.

'What do you think, Gnasher?' he asked his faithful pet. 'Would we rather have veg that never stops growing, veg that are ruthless and super-intelligent, or some kind of living fossil dinosaur veg?'

'**Gnashy-gnish!**' barked Gnasher emphatically, meaning 'anything as long as it tastes of sausages, please!'

'Hi Dennis!' called a familiar voice behind him. It was Dennis's friend, Vito.

OF COURSE! VITO KNOWS EVERYTHING ABOUT THE ENVIRONMENT AND THE PLANET. SHE'LL KNOW WHAT I SHOULD DO!

'Are you going to the allotments?' asked Vito. 'My family has one. We're going to grow all our own organic vegetables, hopefully.'

'Vito,' began Dennis, suddenly nervous as

he realised she probably wouldn't think his idea was a very good one.

'Can I ask you a hyper-critical question?'

Vito nodded. 'I think you mean a hypothetical question, but whatever.'

> A hypothetical question is one that relates to things that are possible or could happen, not actual things that have happened – Helpful Ed.

'Would you use a super-growth serum on your allotment?'

Vito shook her head. 'No way! I don't believe in meddling with nature. We only use natural fertilisers on our allotment, and we don't use pesticide. We don't know what artificial chemicals might do to the environment or even to our bodies.'

Dennis looked downcast. 'Not even a

teeny-weeny bit of super-growth juice?'

'Not if super-growth juice even existed,' said Vito firmly.

'Maybe you're right,' said Dennis. 'Maybe I shouldn't turbocharge my turnips with the prof's magic growth formula.'

THE QUESTION NOW IS... WHERE HAVE THEY GONE?

Vito stopped walking. 'Was that really a hypothetical question, Dennis?'

But Dennis and Gnasher were gone – again!

Once he was back at the allotment, Dennis stashed the jars in the greenhouse.

Sometimes, when people disagree with

Dennis, he has trouble understanding them.
He never has that problem with Gnasher. They
understand each other perfectly.

WHAT NOW, GNASHER?

Bin the turbo juice, Dennis.

I DON'T THINK VITO WAS 100%
CONVINCED USING THE PROF'S
FORMULA WAS A GOOD IDEA.

She thought it
was more barking than
Battersea Dogs'
Home!

BUT I'M MILES BEHIND EVERYONE
ELSE IN THE CONTEST.

Sometimes you
have to work hard for
things. that's just a lesson
you'll have to learn the
hard way.

WHAT DO YOU THINK WE SHOULD DO?

See? Dennis knows **EXACTLY** what Gnasher is thinking! Well, almost . . .

'Okay, let's see,' said Dennis. 'The prof's formula kind of worked twice, then didn't work. That means the missing ingredient was in the first two but not the third. So if I mix the first two formulas together, that will work! Well, probably.'

'What's the worst that can happen?'

'**Gnash gnash!**' said Gnasher. *I guess we're about to find out.*

'I don't have any sausages, Gnasher,' said Dennis, almost understanding.

Gnasher sighed, then lay down to watch. Life was never dull with Dennis around!

Dennis grabbed the old watering can from the potting bench and poured the contents of the first jar into it, then whatever was in the second.

He carefully dribbled a little of the mixture over the soil where his seeds were planted. Nothing happened.

Then he went back and poured on some more. Nothing.

Dennis poured the mixture onto the

ground until it formed a puddle, then took a
step backwards.

Still nothing . . .

There was a flash of light and a minor
earthquake. Dennis landed on his back in the
dirt beside Gnasher, who felt a bit smug that
he'd already hit the deck.

Scrambling to his feet, Dennis inspected the soil.

Absolutely nothing!

Disheartened, Dennis dusted himself down, replaced the watering can on the potting bench.

'Maybe you were right, Gnasher,' he said. 'We need to use all three mixtures.'

He took the lid off the last jar of growth serum and allowed a couple of drops to fall onto a small patch of earth.

'I'll try it on this one little area,' said Dennis. 'And if that doesn't work, I'll just have to have a better idea tomorrow!'

'**Gnasha-gnashee-gnoo!**' barked Gnasher. *Whatever tomorrow's idea is, It definitely can't be any worse than today's!*

'No, Gnasher, I still don't have any sausages,' said Dennis, and they headed for home.

Chapter Five

WHAT'S TOMATO WITH YOU?

Dennis couldn't sleep. He looked at his alarm

clock. It was 03:17 in the morning.

It felt like he'd been awake all night.

Gnasher snored at the bottom of the bed, where he lay on Dennis's feet. Dennis could feel his wiry body rising and falling as he breathed. Every now and again, his legs would twitch, as if he'd just surprised a postman in Dreamland.

Every time Dennis nodded off, he woke up with a start from the same dream. He was down at the allotment and the growth serums had done something after all.

His veggies were spectacular. They were the Seven Veggie Wonders of the World!!

It's no good, thought Dennis. *I can't wait till morning to have a look at my veg.*

He jumped out of bed, pulled on his clothes and sneaked out of the house with Gnasher. He grabbed his skateboard from its parking space

THE SEVEN VEGGIE WONDERS OF THE WORLD

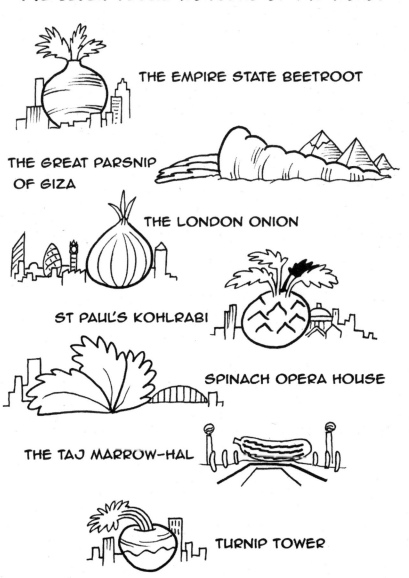

THE EMPIRE STATE BEETROOT

THE GREAT PARSNIP OF GIZA

THE LONDON ONION

ST PAUL'S KOHLRABI

SPINACH OPERA HOUSE

THE TAJ MARROW-HAL

TURNIP TOWER

next to Dad's car, jumped on and turned left on to Gasworks Road.

Two minutes later, including a quick bash on the halfpipe at the skatepark, Dennis arrived at the allotments. Everything was quiet, but Gnasher growled.

Dennis dropped to one knee beside him. 'What is it, Gnasher?'

'That came from over where my plot is!' cried Dennis, sprinting into the allotments.

He hurdled over fences, burst through bushes and slid under gates. When he got to his plot, he gawped.

'My greenhouse!' he said. 'Someone's broken in!'

Dennis looked inside. Nothing. Just a hole in the ground where he'd poured on those few drops of the third serum.

'Someone's stolen my vegetables!' he cried.

He looked around, hoping to catch the thief

red-handed. The dirty greenhouse glass made it hard to see, but then . . . a movement in the next plot over!

'Come on, Gnasher!' Dennis shouted. 'It's the thief!'

He ran outside, knocking the last jar of growth formula over as he went.

The liquid slowly trickled out of the jar and pooled on the ground, before disappearing under the surface.

He's headed for the exit! thought Dennis.

The thief was fast! Dennis could see a body smashing its way through the undergrowth at top speed. He could hear Gnasher panting as he chased.

'Follow him, Gnasher!' he hissed. 'I'll head him off at the gates!'

Dennis decided he could only get to the gates first if he went cross-country. He veered off the path into an allotment and carried on as fast as he could.

SQUELCH! went a marrow!

SPLUDGE! went a pumpkin!

And ***SQUIRT!*** went several ears
of sweetcorn.

Dennis turned back onto the path just
in time to block the gates. As he listened to
the approaching noise on the allotments, he
thought to himself, *I bet it's Walter!*

But it wasn't.

A figure skidded round the corner and
stopped when it saw Dennis.

'**OMG**!' said Dennis. He'd wanted to catch
the thief red-handed, but he didn't expect to
catch him red-FACED!

Glaring at Dennis and breathing hard, was

a giant **TOMATO**!

It was taller than Dennis and twice as grumpy as a hungry Abyssinian wire-haired tripe hound.

'**Crumbs!**' said Dennis. 'I'm not sure if it was such a good idea to **KETCHUP** with you after all!'

The tomato grinned evilly and took an ominous step towards Dennis.

'**GNASH-GNASH-GNASH!**' barked Gnasher as he emerged from the allotments at top tripe-hound speed.

The tomato was startled. It looked at the incoming hound, then turned back to Dennis and said, 'I'll be back!'

Then the tomato turned and ran, crashing straight through the allotment fence as though it were made of matchsticks.

Dennis rubbed his eyes. He was still in bed, right? Dreaming?

He pinched himself.

'**OW**!' Nope!

Gnasher was sniffing around the splintered remains of the fence where the terrifying tomato had broken through.

'Good boy, Gnasher,' said Dennis, stroking

his loyal pal. 'You got me out of a bit of

bother there!'

Chapter Six

THE BLAME GAME

The sun was almost up when Dennis and Gnasher got back to their greenhouse, where another surprise was waiting for them!

The hole the freaky tomato had dug itself up from was still there, but incredibly, the rest of Dennis's veg had sprouted and were looking FANTASTIC!

VEGGIE-LICIOUS!

'None of this was even above the ground when we chased that tomato, Gnasher,' said Dennis. 'And now look! What's going on around here?'

He picked up the empty growth serum jars and examined them.

'Nah!' he decided. 'I'm just an awesome gardener! I've got green fingernails, or whatever it is they say!'

'That tomato must have just been a rogue bad seed.'

Soon, more gardeners started to arrive at the allotments, and no one was very happy about what had happened overnight.

'My majestic military marrow!' cried the Colonel, Dennis's next-door neighbour. 'It's been smashed . . . to a pulp!

'My sweetcorn!' yelled Butch Butcher. 'It was as tall as me yesterday and now look – it's all shook up!'

'And something has pulverised my prize pumpkin!' growled Grizzly Griller, the Beanotown TV survival expert. 'If I had to guess, I'd say it was a bear, or possibly an Abominable Snowmenace! I wish I'd been here. I know exactly how to subdue a hungry bear!'

'It wasn't a grizzly bear,' said Dennis. 'I saw what did it.'

The Colonel, Butch and Grizzly looked at him curiously.

'Your veggies were splatteroonied by a giant evil tomato who could walk and talk.'

When Dennis said it aloud, it sounded a
little far-fetched.

YOU DO KNOW THAT
SOUNDS A LITTLE WEIRD?

'A giant tomato?' said the Colonel with
an incredulous laugh.

'That could walk and talk?' spluttered
Grizzly. 'I've never heard of such a thing!'

'Are you sure it wasn't nuthin' but a
hound dog?' asked Butch Butcher, eyeing
Gnasher suspiciously.

'That's the truth,' said Dennis. 'Come on, Gnasher. Let's go.'

Back at Dennis's plot, Vito, Pie Face and Rubi were waiting. Dennis told his friends what had happened. Well, not *everything* that had happened, but most of it.

'The logical explanation is that you dreamed the whole thing,' said Rubi.

'And then sleep-stomped all the veg,' said Pie Face.

Vito just looked at Dennis. 'Is there something you aren't telling us, Dennis?'

ER... UM... WELL...

Just then, the Colonel, Butch and Grizzly appeared again, this time with Sergeant Slipper in tow.

'Dennis,' began the Colonel, 'I wonder if you would explain to Sergeant Slipper what it is that you saw last night?'

Dennis sighed. 'When I got here before dawn, there was a giant tomato squishing around. Gnasher and I chased him but he got away. He trampled all the veg while he was running.'

Sergeant Slipper looked dubious.

A GIANT TOMATO?

YES. IT WAS TOM-ENDOUS!

'I can give you a description if you like,' added Dennis. 'My friend Khadira could do one of those photofits for you. She's so good at drawing, we call her Sketch Khad.'

'So you got a look at the culprit's face?' said Slipper, getting out his notebook. 'What did it look like?'

'Red. Like a tomato. Only with a face. And arms and legs. It told me it would be back.'

Sergent Slipper didn't seem convinced. 'And did it say *when* it would be back?'

'It was more of a threat,' said Dennis, 'than something to put in your diary.'

DENNIS WOULDN'T LIE ABOUT SOMETHING LIKE THIS!

CAN I TAKE A LOOK AT YOUR SHOES, PLEASE?

Dennis didn't like the way this conversation was going. This was sus!

'Why?' he said hotly. 'Why do you want to see them?'

'There may be evidence to show us who the culprit was,' said Slipper.

Dennis shrugged. He was innocent, so he had nothing to worry about. Right?

Dennis lifted his foot from the ground so everyone could examine the evidence. There was A LOUD GASP.

Dennis's trainers were dripping with gloop. Marrow juice. Sweetcorn kernels. Pumpkin seeds. It was like something Olive the dinner lady would serve for school dinner. And she'd call it Guilty Stew!

Sergeant Slipper whipped the suspect shoe off, leaving Dennis to hop on one leg, and strode off as purposefully as he could, followed by everyone else. At the Colonel's plot, he laid Dennis's trainer in the mangled marrow. It fitted like Cinderella's foot in a glass slipper, only it was Dennis's stinky trainer in a mashed marrow.

GASP!

WILL YOU LOT STOP GASPING? IT'S ACTUALLY QUITE FRIGHTENING.

Slipper turned to Dennis. 'The evidence clearly suggests it was your foot that mushed this marrow, Dennis. What have you got to say for yourself?'

'Er, can I have my trainer back, I guess?' Slipper shook his head. This was not the answer he was looking for.

Dennis flushed.

'It . . . it was quite dark, and I was chasing the tomato. Maybe I did stand on the marrow. But I didn't do it on purpose!'

'But why didn't this giant, evil tomato leave any footprints then?' asked Butch. He was right, the tomato had left no trail other than the destruction it had caused.

'And why didn't it destroy any of YOUR vegetables,' said Grizzly, accusingly. 'All your veg seem to be doing very nicely indeed!'

Dennis had no answers to their questions.

Sergeant Slipper snapped his notebook shut and pocketed it. 'I can't prove you did this, Dennis, but I can arrest you to protect what's left of my vegetables!'

'Actually, you can't do that,' said Rubi. Sergeant Slipper glared at her.

The grown-ups walked away, casting reproachful backward glances at Dennis as they went.

'You guys believe me, right?' Dennis asked his friends.

SUSPICION!

'Of course,' said Rubi. 'But you have to admit it looks bad, Dennis.'

'When the allotments were opened, you told everyone you'd rather mash a potato than plant one,' said Pie Face, not very helpfully. 'And that you'd love to turn the tables on an onion for once and make IT cry. And that the only good carrot was stuck in a snowman's face. And . . .'

'Those were jokes, Pie Face!' said Dennis. 'No one was meant to take them seriously!'

'But you did say them, and now you say that a giant tomato-man came into the allotments at night, mashing, smashing and squishing the best vegetables, leaving yours alone,' said Rubi.

OOPS! ME AND MY BIG MOUTH . . . THE VEGE-TABLES HAVE TURNED!

'The day after a big prize is announced for the best veg, and Dennis wants to win really badly but he's miles behind everybody else!' said Pie Face, even less helpfully. 'It all fits . . .'

...WELL, IT WOULD, IF WE DIDN'T BELIEVE YOU.

THANKS GUYS!

'Thank you for believing in me,' said Dennis. 'I'm innocent, and I'm going to prove it! Right, Gnasher?'

'Gnash-gnash!' barked Gnasher. He knew Dennis was innocent, and he wouldn't rest until the whole world knew it too.

Chapter Seven

WITH COUSINS LIKE MINNIE, WHO NEEDS ENEMIES?

Dennis couldn't bear to hang around the allotments for long. So many people were picking up their crushed or spoiled vegetables, casting accusing glances at him.

He and Gnasher wandered home, climbed the conker tree in the back garden and let themselves into Dennis's tree house.

The Tree House (or 'Special Branch HQ' as Dennis calls it!) Can you spot the secret trapdoor?

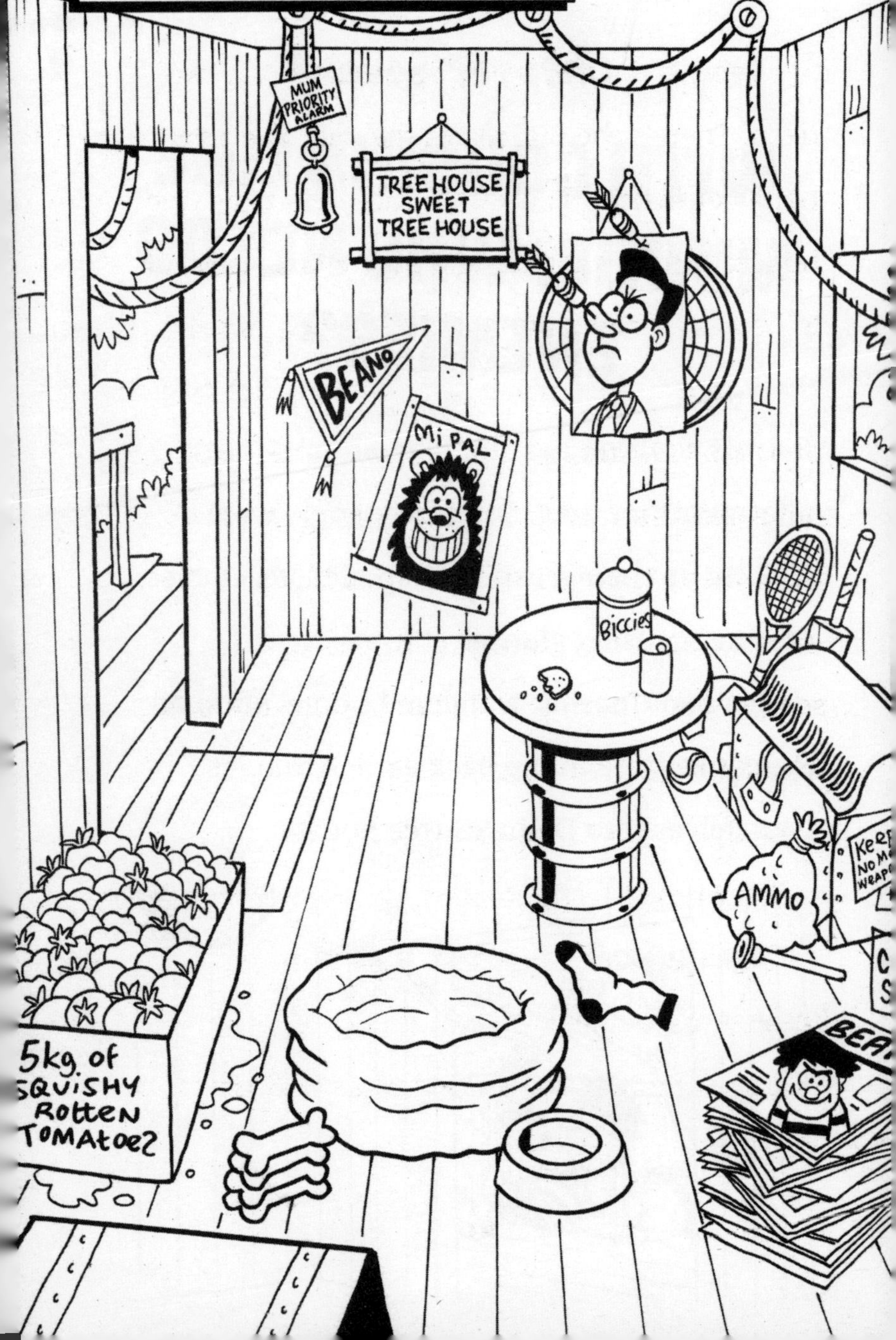
MUM PRIORITY ALARM
TREE HOUSE SWEET TREE HOUSE
BEANO
Mi PAL
Biccies
AMMO
5kg of SQUISHY Rotten TOMAtoeS

Dennis is really lucky because he has two dens. There's the big one in the woods where he hangs out with his friends, and there's his tree house, which is the den he uses when he wants to be alone. Well, alone with Gnasher, obvs!

'We need a plan,' he said, patting Gnasher on the head. 'We need to find out what's going on at the allotments. Is it something to do with the growth formula, do you think?'

Gnasher rolled his eyes. But at least it seemed like Dennis was starting to work out where things had gone wrong.

A figure appeared at the door.

'Hi Minnie,' said Dennis.

'I heard what happened,' said Minnie. 'I knew you'd be here.'

She sat down and tickled Gnasher's paws.

'Why did you do it?' she asked. Minnie doesn't bother with small talk. She just gets straight to the point.

'I didn't!' said Dennis.

'Come on, Dennis,' said Minnie. 'It's me, your cousin!

'Did you come here just to make me feel better?' asked Dennis sarcastically.

'No one believes me,' he carried on. 'Rubi, Vito and Pie Face say they do, but I think they feel like they have to say that. Even <u>YOU</u> don't believe me.'

Minnie stroked her chin. 'What about fingerprints? Did they dust the place? That could get you off the hook. If you're innocent, that is . . .'

'Everything's been cleaned up,' said Dennis, shaking his head.

'CCTV?'

'Nope.'

'Amateurs!' groaned Minnie. 'Don't they know anything?'

'Well, you'll just have to take my word for it,' said Dennis. 'I didn't do it.'

Minnie looked at him, then took quite a large box from under her jersey.

'A lie detector?' said Dennis, outraged. 'I'm not taking a lie-detector test!'

Minnie pushed the box to one side
with a regretful look.

'How about a pinky promise?' she said.

Dennis sighed. 'I pinky promise I did not
rampage around the allotments smashing
veg in the middle of the night to sabotage the
competition and that I definitely did see a giant
tomato do it before it ran away.'

'Well, why didn't you just say so?' cried
Minnie. 'I always knew you were innocent!'

Dennis was speechless.

'There's only one way you can prove your
innocence,' said Minnie. 'You have to catch
the real parp in the ect. I mean, the real perp
in the act. I've watched enough true-crime
documentaries to know that criminals always
return to the scene of the crime.'

And THAT's why Dennis and Gnasher found
themselves sneaking out of the house under
cover of darkness for the second night in a row.

Only this time, they wouldn't be alone. Minnie was coming too.

But no amount of company could prepare them for what they found when they got to the allotments!

Chapter Eight

THE VEG WHO LIVED

Dennis's vegetable patch was ablaze!

A bonfire made of wooden tool handles crackled, throwing orange flames high into the sky. Dancing around it were a fiendish mob of . . . GIANT VEGETABLES!

Peering through a gap in the fence, Dennis recognised his tomato nemesis from the night before, but now there were even more giant vegetables, including a pumpkin, a carrot, a parsnip, mushrooms and – UGH! – Brussels sprouts!

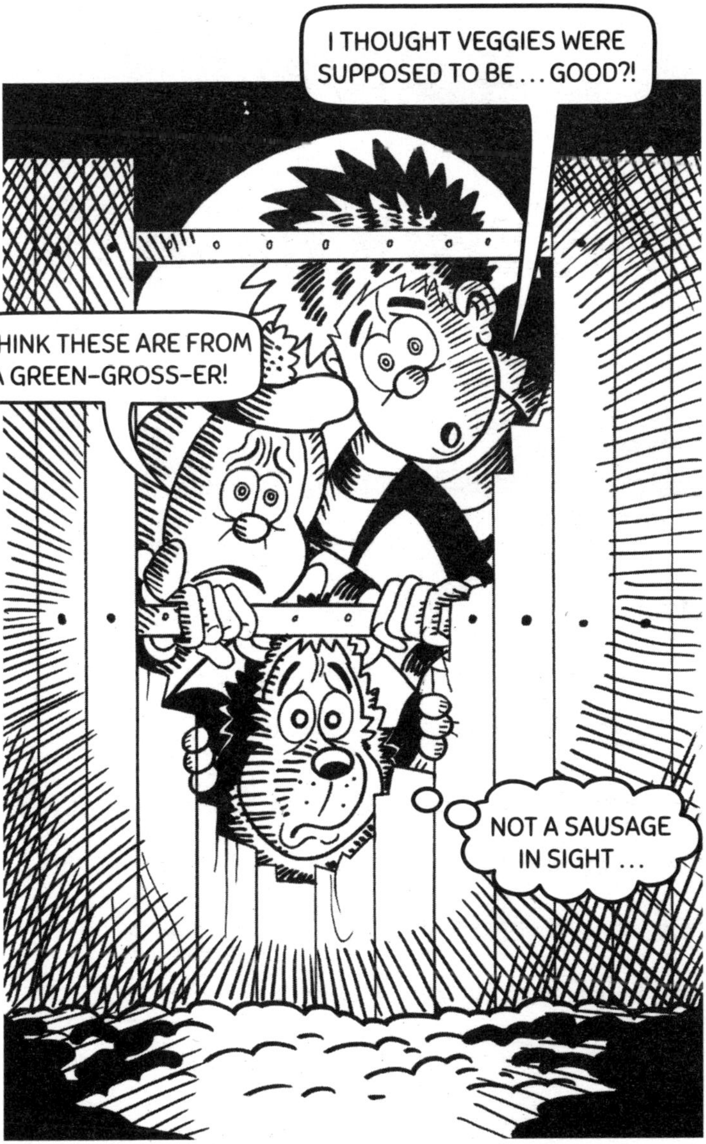
I THOUGHT VEGGIES WERE SUPPOSED TO BE . . . GOOD?!
I THINK THESE ARE FROM A GREEN-GROSS-ER!
NOT A SAUSAGE IN SIGHT . . .

'OMG!' whispered Minnie. 'You were telling the truth!'

'I thought you believed me!' hissed Dennis. 'What about my pinky promise?'

'Pinky-shminky!' said Minnie.

They were silent once more, watching the infernal vegetables as they danced around the bonfire.

'Listen!' whispered Minnie. 'Are . . . are they singing?'

They were.

'It . . . it sounds familiar,' said Dennis, puzzled. 'Almost . . . happy.'

At the end of the song, the evil veggies stomped on some poor, unsuspecting non-zombie veg, pulping it instantly.

The pumpkin raised his hands to the sky and proclaimed, 'Tonight is the night of the living veg! Tonight is the night when we take our revenge! But first . . .'

He looked down at his expectant army of awful associates.

'VEGGIE CONGA!'

And, with that, the horrid, living list of ingredients formed a line behind the pumpkin and conga'd their way into the night, singing as they went.

It took a moment for Minnie and Dennis to catch their breath. Finally, they snuck into Dennis's patch, made their way around the still-lit bonfire and into the greenhouse.

Minnie picked up the knocked-over growth-formula jars and eyed the holes in the ground where the awful vegetables had apparently come from. Then she looked at Dennis.

DOO-DOO-DOO! COME DO THE VEGGIE CONGA! OO-OO-OO, IT'S VEGGIE NIGHT FOR SURE...

IS THERE SOMETHING YOU'RE NOT TELLING ME? HOW COME IT'S YOUR PLOT THAT HAS ALL THESE ZOMBIE VEGETABLES DANCING AND SINGING IN IT?

Dennis gulped. It was time to come clean.

'Well,' he said. 'I might have got some experimental growth formula from the prof, mixed it all together and slapped the whole lot over my seeds.'

'If I remember rightly, there was one that

made veg grow forever, one that made them super-intelligent and ruthless, and one that was based on dinosaur DNA. That one had a missing ingredient though.'

'Not missing any more, I bet,' said Minnie.

'I guess this is all my fault,' said Dennis. 'Everyone told me I should be patient, but I had to find a shortcut.'

Gnasher licked Dennis's hand. *Yes, yes, it is your fault. But I love you anyway.*

'Don't blame yourself,' said Minnie. 'That's exactly what I would have done. Only I'd have done it in someone else's greenhouse, so the crime couldn't be traced back to me. I'm smarter than you, see?'

Dennis's phone pinged. Rubi was on group chat.

Rubi: U know that tomato u were talking about earlier? I think I just saw it. And he's got friends!

Rubi: I can see them from my bedroom window. What's going on?

Stevie: I just saw a gang of ugly veg walking down MY street. Is this real?

Vito: OMG! A bunch of humongous greens are running past my house?

Pie Face: Am I dreaming, or did the filling for the biggest veggie pie in history just conga through my garden?

Dennis: Keep calm, everyone! I'll explain later.

'Bad news,' said Dennis, putting his phone back in his pocket.

'I know,' said Minnie, looking at her own phone. 'I got the messages too. Let's see. Rubi saw them first, then Stevie, Vito, then Pie Face. That means they're headed for the town centre.'

'If they've gone the long way round, maybe we can take a shortcut and intercept them,' said Dennis.

'That's a bad idea,' said Minnie. 'I say we take a shortcut and intercept them.'

Dennis sighed. 'Good idea, cuz.'

Chapter Nine

IT'LL ALL WORK OUT IN THE BLEND ... RIGHT?

They parkoured like the wind, leaping kerbs, somersaulting over fences, rolling as they landed to help them on their way.

As they neared the town centre, they could hear glass smashing and the sound of demonic vegetables laughing.

IS THAT THE SOUND OF DEMONIC VEGETABLES LAUGHING?

If you can't imagine what that sounds like, it goes something like this:

BWAA-HA-HA-HA-HURR-HURR-HURR!

They ducked out of sight and peered round the corner to get a look at what was happening.

'They've broken into Rocket Man!' said Minnie. 'But why?'

Rocket Man was a vegetarian delicatessen that specialised in salads. Its owner, Veg Dwight, grew all his own produce ethically, organically and enthusiastically.

The vegetable army were dragging boxes of salad leaves, pomegranates and tomatoes out of the store, then devouring them as fast as they could.

'They're eating all the salad,' said Dennis, puzzled. 'Does that make them cannibals?'

'The worst kind,' said Minnie. 'Vege-bals!'

'Hi guys!' a voice said behind them, causing Minnie to leap into Dennis's arms and Dennis to leap into Gnasher's.

'Show yourself, whoever you are!' said

Minnie. 'And eat the boy first!'

Minne had nothing to worry about though,

as it was just Stevie and Vito.

Gnasher let Dennis down, then Dennis let

Minnie down.

'We shall never speak of this again,' said

Minnie gravely.

'Agreed,' said Dennis, then turned to Stevie and Vito.

'What are you two doing here?' he asked.

'We came out to see if we could help,' said Vito. 'Seems like there's a bit of a disaster going on down here.'

'Actually,' said Stevie. 'I'm here to film the creepy zombie vegetables smashing up the town. This is You-Hoo gold! This is definitely going viral!'

'**Drat!** I wish I'd thought of that,' muttered Minnie. Her mobile was almost out of juice.

'This has got something to do with that growth formula, hasn't it?' Vito asked.

Dennis nodded. 'Yes, but I'm going to fix it,' he said.

'**WE'RE** going to fix it,' Vito corrected. 'It

doesn't matter whose fault this is, we all have to help. Why don't you fill us in on the details?'

When Dennis had explained how it had all happened, Vito looked thoughtful.

'If bad science created these monsters, maybe good science can defeat them!'

'To the Top Secret Research Station!' cried Stevie.

'Wait!' hissed Minnie, hauling them all back into the shadows.

The vile vegetables were coming their way!

The friends shrank back, hoping the motley crew of edible evil wouldn't see them.

The pumpkin raised his arms and the other veg fell silent.

'Fellow foodstuffs, the hour of our dreams is approaching,' it boomed. 'With every vegetable we consume, we grow stronger!'

'General Parsnip!' the pumpkin bellowed. 'Are you ready?'

'Yes, Optimus Pumpkin,' answered the parsnip obediently.

'And you, Commander Carrot? Are the Sprout Scouts prepared to fight the food fight?'

'Tom Tooter, Frank Farter and Brenda Botty-Burp! Atten-shun!' Commander Carrot screeched at three mischievous-looking Brussels sprouts.

The sprouts quickly stood to attention, saluting their orange leader, then each other, then Optimus Pumpkin and then Commander Carrot again, before dissolving into fits of cackling giggles.

The pumpkin glared at the sprouts, who hid behind Commander Carrot.

'We're ready,' sighed Commander Carrot, clearly groaning inside.

'Red Team Leader,' the giant gourd-for-nothing pumpkin boomed. 'I hope the Mushroom Mob are more disciplined?'

The tomato Dennis had chased the night before cracked its heels together and saluted.

'Sir, yes sir!' said the tomato.

Three little mushrooms moved like ninjas into cool, ready-for-action poses.

Optimus Pumpkin drew himself up to his full height.

'You all know the plan! Leave no fruit unsquished, no vegetable uneaten! Then bring me the leader of this town so I can make him an offer he can't refuse. We will not be pushed around any longer – the rise of the vegetables has begun!'

'Tomorrow, we will rule Beanotown! And then, the world is our oyster mushroom! The puny humans cannot stop us! At my command, unleash OPERATION RATATOUILLE!'

Then, with a shriek like Dad makes when the shower goes cold, the veg sprinted off in different directions to do their worst.

'PHEW!' said Minnie. 'All they want

IT'S A VEGETABLE RAMPAGE!

is the mayor. They can have him.'

'Didn't you hear?' asked Stevie. 'They want
to rule us all. Probably with an iron fist.'

'Vegetables are a really good source of iron,'
said Vito. 'Especially green ones.'

'Well, thanks for that,
Mrs Brightside,' said Minnie. 'I'll bear that in
mind next time one tries to
eat me!'

YOU DO REALISE
THAT AFTER I
EAT YOU I'LL BE
STRONGER THAN
EVER?

'Come on, guys. This is serious,' said Dennis. 'I know this is mostly – about 51% - my fault, but I can't stop them alone. I need your help. Are you in?'

Minnie instantly fist-bumped Dennis. In the ribs.

'I'm in!' she said.

OH, GOODY!

Vito nodded. 'I'm in.'

Dennis turned to Stevie. 'What about you? Will you help us?'

'Are you kidding?' said Stevie, checking to make sure his phone had plenty of battery left. 'I'll never get a chance at a billion views again!'

Dennis grinned. He loved it when the gang came together!

'Minnie and Stevie – follow that pumpkin. I want to know where he is when the time comes to deal with him. If we can defeat him, the rest of those nasty veg will be toast!'

'Soup,' said Minnie. 'They'll be soup, Dennis, not toast.'

'We're gonna need a bigger stock cube,' said Vito drily.

'Come on, Stevie,' Minnie said, and off they ran.

Vito looked at Dennis.

'Science?' she asked.

'Science,' agreed Dennis.

Professor Von Screwtop was in his pyjamas and dressing gown when they got to the Top Secret Research Station. He liked to go to bed early and get up early as he did his best thinking before the sun came up. Rubi was watching TV.

'So my growth formula actually worked?' he asked, once Dennis had explained what was going on.

'Well, I don't know if you could really say it *worked*,' said Dennis. 'I basically mixed them all up and threw the lot on my veg. And then this.'

VERY INTERESTING... MAYBE WITH A FEW LITTLE TWEAKS...

'We need to know how to kill the veg,' said Vito, interrupting. 'How do we reverse your formula's effects?'

The professor stood up and grabbed a marker from the shelf below his whiteboard. It had lots of writing on it under a title, THE MEANING OF LIFE.

The prof started to wipe the board clean.

'I can think of three ways to kill supersized zombie vegetables,' he said, starting to make a list.

'Dad . . .' said Rubi.

'One.' The prof continued wiping. 'A supersized food processor, or maybe a soup pot.'

'Dad!' said Rubi, louder.

'Two: supersized zombie bugs to eat the veg, if you can find some. '

'**DAD**!' yelled Rubi.

'Not now, Rubidium!' said the professor, working the cloth right into the corners of the whiteboard. 'And three: just wait for them to go mouldy and throw them on the zombie compost heap. That's the circle of life, and it moves us all.'

He turned to Rubi. 'Now, Rubi. What is it?'

'I was going to ask if you had made a copy of your solution to the meaning of life?' said Rubi, exasperated. 'Because you just wiped it right off your whiteboard!'

The professor turned pale.

Vito groaned.

'But we don't have a giant soup pot, blender, zombie bugs or much time,' she said. 'Isn't there another way?'

'Don't worry!' said Dennis, abruptly. 'Thanks for trying, Prof. We'll be off now.'

'Yes, you're welcome,' said the professor. 'Come on, Rubidium, it's well past my bedtime. I have to work out the meaning of life . . . again!'

But Rubi was gone, along with Vito and Dennis.

And so were the last remaining jars of Professor Von Screwtop's failed attempts to create a super-quick, super-size vegetable growth formula.

Chapter Ten

THE WIDL PROBLEM!

Rubi's eyes narrowed as she looked at Dennis.
Uh Oh!

'I. Can't. Believe. You. Did. This!' Rubi
shouted. 'You used the super-growth serums
to win a stupid gardening contest?!'

Dennis realised he was going to have to
explain himself.

The pressure was on. He needed to wing it
like a politician – they were able to get away
with anything with some smooth talk!

'Er, it wasn't me,' offered Dennis.

'Vito?' began Rubi. 'Is Dennis currently holding three jars we both just witnessed him nab from my dad's lab?'

'Yes, m'lud. I do believe he is,' nodded Vito. The verdict was in.

'GUILTY! You've already unleashed chaos with the first batch. But, when the compost settles on this, it'll be Dad who goes to jail! And that's the best-case scenario!'

Dennis had his head bowed; Vito wondered if Rubi had been too harsh?

Nope. Dennis slowly looked up, revealing a massive grin, like the star of a toothpaste ad. Vito could have sworn she spotted a flash followed by a fresh TING sound.

'OK, I am guilty. Guilty of having a BLAMAZING plan to save Beanotown . . .'

He explained that, while Rubi had been distracted trying to stop her dad destroying his meaning of life research, he'd been listening very carefully. The prof had revealed a safe, and ecologically sound way to get the veg back under control.

'Leaving them to turn into compost!' said Vito, realising that, for once, Dennis had listened and learned.

'Nah, I mean the supersized veg-eating bugs!' said Dennis, looking up from frantically typing messages into the group chat.

Vito and Rubi gawped at Dennis, but before they'd time to protest, he outlined the next stage of his plan.

'Don't just stand there, guys! That's Plan C. We're about to activate Plan A.'

Rubi's frown deepened as Dennis continued his plotting. 'Optimus Pumpkin can be stopped by teamwork. I've messaged Stevie to try to lure Commander Carrot and his Sprout Scouts to the Top Secret Research Station.'

'Wait! Your *plan* is to lure them to the place where my dad is sleeping?!'

Thanks to Stevie's competitive parents constantly battling it out to become his favourite, he had *all* the gear. he needed to pull his mission off.

He was currently wearing a headband with a small camera attached to the front, with another at the back. He called it his chase-cam. He'd blagged some great footage already, capturing a pack of angry veg chasing him into Beanotown's 24-hour supermarket, Widl.

Now he was in hiding, squished underneath some shelving holding a weird collection of random stuff that seemed to have been delivered to the wrong shop.

IT'S AMAZING WHAT YOU CAN BUY IN WIDL!

He'd messaged Dennis to ask whether there was a Plan B. As he typed, he could hear the carrots and sprouts topping up their iron levels via the vulnerable leafy veggies in the fresh produce aisle. Stevie was worried. He'd lured the veggies to an all-you-can-eat buffet!

He knew he had to get them to the lab, but how? He reached up and rummaged through the racks above to see if there was anything that could help him. Maybe he'd discover something he could use to batter his way through the veggies? Two minutes later, a sweaty Stevie was, clutching a giant inflatable sausage.

HMM... NOT EXACTLY WHAT I WAS LOOKING FOR!

He'd also discovered an electric scooter! Stevie fired it up, and, waving the sausage like a medieval jouster to clear a path, he was soon back on the road. Even better, the veggies followed in hot pursuit, all the way to the Top Secret Research Station. The footage was going to be incredible!

And, if he was lucky, Stevie would turn out to be inedible!

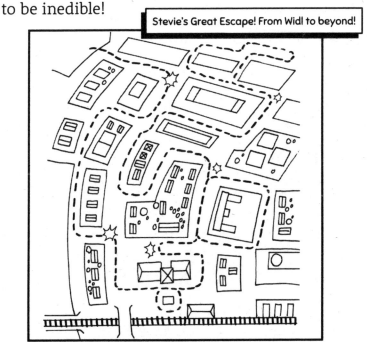

Stevie's Great Escape! From Widl to beyond!

Dennis and Rubi were ready and waiting beside Rubi's hot tub.

'Have you turned the hot tub heat up to the max, Rubes?' asked Dennis.

'I've activated the thermal override. I normally use it like a warm bath, to help relax my muscles. But I think mutant veg would *relax* permanently at about 100 degrees hotter, by my calculations,' Rubi replied.

They heard a low hum in the distance. As it got louder, they could hear Stevie yelling, 'Smile for the camera, sweetcorn teeth,' followed by the angry gnashing of vicious veg.

Dennis nodded to Rubi – it was time for their enemy to be Vito-ed!

Outside, Stevie was hurtling down the steep ramp leading into the basement at top speed. He was moving so quickly, it looked like he was jet-powered. That's what happens when sinister Sprout Scouts start nipping at your ankles . . .

Stevie gunned it down the ramp aiming for the open door, and then – uh-oh! Like many Widl FOMO* bargains, the batteries had run out! The scooter started to slow. Stevie put his foot down and shoved with all his might. And

*Fear Of Missing Out – Helpful Ed.

again. He was powered purely by FOBE** now!

Stevie caught a glimpse of Vito who was holding a remote control, ready to slam the door shut as soon as he was safe. He wondered how good her sense of timing was as the doors started to close when he approached them . . .

**Fear Of Being Eaten - Even-more-helpful Ed.

The doors slammed shut, bursting the sausage explosively, before the veg could catch up. It was a classic Beano banger and smash!

'Hey, what's the difference between bogeys and sprouts?' Vito called to the gathered veggies, who were furious that Stevie had disappeared.

Commander Carrot and the Sprout Scouts stopped dead.

'We don't know,' the sprouts hissed angrily as one. 'What is the difference between bogeys and sprouts?'

'Some kids will eat bogeys.'

A strange squeal, like a hundred little tyres screeching, came from the assembled sprouts. They hadn't enjoyed the punchline.

'Tough crowd!' muttered Vito.

I DON'T GET IT.

THAT'S BECAUSE THE JOKE'S ON US! WE'VE BEEN SPROUTWITTED!

She continued to goad them, enjoying herself. 'So much for you little weeds being the muscles from Brussels!'

Result! They turned and chased after Vito.

Vito ran as fast as she could through the professor's lab, down the corridor to the toilets and on towards a set of double doors, which she smashed through without hesitating!

The ground disappeared beneath her feet and as she hurtled into space, she grabbed a dangling rope and held on tight with one hand!

Vito knew what she was doing as she swung gracefully over a boiling hot tub, which had been pushed underneath the platform the doors opened onto. Vito theatrically crumbled a giant stock cube over the water, flexing her forearm as she sprinkled, so the herbs were

evenly spread. She
let go and dropped
smoothly onto a crash mat, placed
carefully by Dennis and Rubi,
who'd been joined by
an exhausted Stevie.

The first Scout
Sprouts tumbled
straight into the
tub. As they
did so, Dennis
winked at them and
gave a shrill whistle.
It was the signal for

MMM...

Gnasher to appear behind the other veg, like a pirate making his enemies walk the plank. Commander Carrot and the remaining Scout Sprouts were in mid-air above the tub before they knew what had gnashed them!

SOUPER TO SEE YOU!

SPALOOSH!

They tumbled into the broth below.

Rubi, Dennis, Vito, Gnasher and Stevie glanced into the hot tub.

'These veg are no longer evil,' said Vito.

'They're starting to smell . . . sort of delicious,' admitted Rubi.

'You've invented a Hot Tub Soup Machine, Rubi,' said Stevie. He was feeling hungry after all that scooting.

Chapter Eleven

SOUPER TROOPERS!

Commander Carrot and his stinky Sprout Scouts were soup; a surprisingly tasty one too!

Dennis asked, 'What's an evil carrot doing in my soup?'

'Looks like the backstroke!' laughed Stevie.

Vito looked a bit shocked. Normally she loved vegetable soup, but these veggies had been running around like living things only a few minutes ago.

Rubi's latest ingenious invention, the Von Screwtop Hot Tub Soup Machine had been a massive **RESULT!**

The souped-up squad took stock. Optimus Pumpkin, Red Leader and the Ninja Mushrooms would still be sowing havoc. The only question was: where?

'How mush-room does a little fun-guy need to cause trouble?' enquired Dennis.

Rubi interrupted. As always, she'd done her homework. 'Optimus Pumpkin said he wanted to crush the town's leader!'

'So he'll be heading for our den to squish me?!' said Dennis.

'Nope, he's a grown-up gourd, he thinks the mayor is boss. He underestimates us kids . . . which is why we'll get a chance to squish him into pumpkin pie!'

Dennis thought about Pie Face. He owed him a pie for borrowing his skateboard last week.

'Time to get to the Mayor's house. There's not a minute to lose!' he yelled. The chase was on!

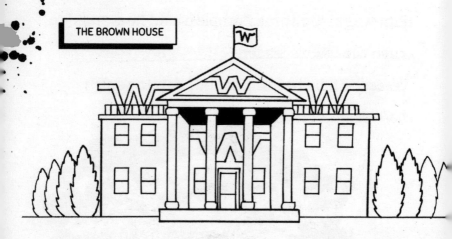

THE BROWN HOUSE

The gang rushed to Gasworks Road, where 'Tranquility' – the fancy villa belonging to Mayor Brown – towered over the surrounding houses. Dennis remembered how Walter always joked that the Menace family home next door looked like a kennel in comparison. Talk about a nasty neighbour!

But something even nastier was moving in today. The Mushroom Mob were approaching the gates in a hurry. Ninja Bill and his twin Phil had taken to beating people with their large caps. Their leader Ninja Jill had even poisoned someone!

Their battle cries, mixed with the alarm sirens, created a funky backing track to their badness. Mayor Brown had made his fortune from a surveillance business, and his own home was a fortress . . . he would be 100% aware he had 'visitors'.

SLAMSQUISHHHH!

A massive metal security door slammed down, squishing Ninja Bill's nose as he tried to scramble through the letter box. There was a squeal of raw rage from the veggies.

Dennis thought he could hear all sorts of crudities – or was it them being chopped into crudités?

Red Leader, the terrible tomato who Dennis

had already encountered, was taking charge of the situation. Standing beside the door, vines grew from his spindly fingers, spreading all over the front of the house. The Browns were in the brown stuff – the yucky kind – and totally trapped.

The Mushroom Mob started to clamber up the tomato vines, attempting to enter through the windows . . . only for more steel shutters to roll down, barring the way. The mayor had designed his house to be Menace-proof, so there was no way some evil veg were going to waltz in.

'**NOTHING** stops a Ninja-shroom!' roared Red Leader, and his troops mushed on. They climbed onto the flat concrete roof, a luxurious sun terrace, dominated by a large letter 'W' picked out with golden tiles in the centre.

The sneaky 'shrooms tore a giant decorative 'W' from the wall and used it it like a crowbar to start slowly prising the tiles off. They were opening the poshest house in the town as if it were a can of vegetable soup!

Red Leader clambered up. He reached the
roof and stamped ferociously upon the W,
cracking several of the expensive tiles. Dennis
and Stevie followed, just in time to see the
most disturbing vision yet.

The terrifying tomato had joined his mob in performing a 'truffle shuffle' – a weird dance that consisted of them shaking their butts and bellies so hard, the whole roof started to wibble and wobble.

'It looks like a sort of battle dance – they're going into a trance!' said Stevie, not taking his eyes away from his handheld camera for a single second. This was more You-Hoo gold.

The giant W below the boogie-ing butts suddenly split in two, opening into a gaping giant mouth . . . and Red Leader disappeared into it!

'**Aargh!** I'm gazpacho!' he cried, as he fell. 'Tell Heinz I love him!'

At the same instant, an exceedingly **SERIOUS** voice boomed out!

YOUR MAYOR IS LEAVING THE BUILDING – PLEASE SHOW YOUR APPRECIATION.

So much for naming the house 'Tranquility'! It was a loudspeaker recording of Wilbur himself! Dennis showed his appreciation by letting out a loud fart.

Things got even noisier as the Ninja
Mushrooms fearlessly followed their leader,
diving after him, mistaking his wail for a
battle cry!

Their angry shouts were drowned out by
a new rising sound.

**THWACK·THWACK·THWACK·
THWACK·THWACK·THWACK...**

It sounded like a cricket bat hitting a ball,
in fact, *lots* of cricket bats hitting *lots* of balls.
Sliced mushrooms started to fly out of the hole
in the roof. Vito sussed what was happening.

'The giant W is the mayor's personal
landing pad! It's amazeballs. Wilbur's family

are escaping vegemageddon in a helicopter!'

'That's NOT a helicopter,' shouted Dennis.

'IT'S A CHOPPER!'

It certainly was!

Wilbur Force One had switched to full power just as Red Leader and the Mushroom Mob had fallen onto the blades. The blades spluttered to a halt, jammed by chopped mushrooms, in a creamed tomato sauce.

Take-off had been taken off the menu.

Vito looked at the mess and shrugged,
'I guess we could give the mushed veg to Olive.
Couldn't make her ratatouille any more evil
than it normally is!'

I'M ALL OUT OF
RATS – PTOOEY!

But she was rudely interrupted by an inhuman cry of rage from inside the helicopter!

The wiper struggled to clear the screen and Dennis nervously peeked in. OMG! An angry, bright-red face stared back. Had Red Leader taken control of the chopper?!

But it wasn't Red Leader, it was a *red-faced leader*. Wilbur Brown was angry and embarrassed. His house had been redecorated in a shade that could be best described as *baby-nappy brown* and his prized helicopter now resembled a food processor.

'This town doesn't even have a helicopter wash!' he said. 'It'll take ages to clean. Better get started, Walter . . . '

Walter protested that it was probably all Dennis and his friends' fault, so it should be them doing the washing-up. But he was too late. The gang had disappeared quicker than croutons at a salad bar.

Chapter Twelve

OH. MY. GREENFINGERS!

Stevie was worried.

When Optimus Pumpkin had unleashed Commander Carrot and the Scout Sprouts on them, Stevie had lured them away. When he left, Minnie had vowed to keep the leader in her sights. But now she was nowhere to be seen and wasn't responding to their messages.

Dennis promised it would be simple to find her. Gnasher stood and sniffed at the air, trying to pick up her scent. Dennis laughed at his pals and pointed over to the nearest

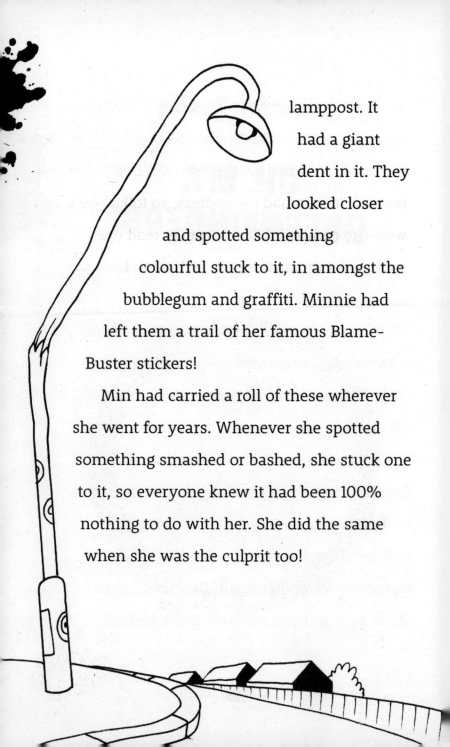

lamppost. It
had a giant
dent in it. They
looked closer
and spotted something
colourful stuck to it, in amongst the
bubblegum and graffiti. Minnie had
left them a trail of her famous Blame-
Buster stickers!

Min had carried a roll of these wherever
she went for years. Whenever she spotted
something smashed or bashed, she stuck one
to it, so everyone knew it had been 100%
nothing to do with her. She did the same
when she was the culprit too!

The stickers each had a picture of Minnie saying: 'It wasn't me!' There was a message in the small print blaming her cousin, Dennis, instead! It even had his address, so folks knew where to complain! Dennis never read the small print on *anything*, so he had no idea . . .

The gang followed the trail to to the allotments. As they approached, Dennis called a sudden halt. He'd spotted a cherry tomato standing lookout on the top of the hedge. He aimed his catapult and scored a direct hit. Only it wasn't a tomato at all. It was the woolly pom-pom on top of Minnie's beret!

Her full head popped up, pea shooter at the ready, and rotated like a tank gun ready to retaliate, before she spotted her guilty cousin and the rest of the gang. She shot Dennis a glare, then gestured for them all to zip it!

SHH!

They heard a low chorus.

♪ ♫ ♪ **'All we are saying . . . is give peas a chance.'** ♫ ♪

'They want to make peace,' smiled a relieved-looking Vito. Minnie shot her an even grumpier glare than she'd fired at Dennis and nodded urgently, urging them to peek over the hedge.

Optimus Pumpkin was wearing a dramatic cape (he'd picked it up in Widl), which swirled as he conducted a choir of very vocal veg. All around him, a variety of vegetables were singing, while gleefully stamping upon pea pods, using them like mini bazookas! The mean, green flying machines were shooting off everywhere.

The kids had to duck to avoid being

podded! When they looked up, they saw
Optimus Pumpkin grab a sorry-looking onion
by the stalk – the type that lies at the back
of the kitchen cupboard, forgotten until the
spring clean. The pumpkin paused, lowered
the onion behind his back, and then farted
on it! The onion was enveloped in a cloud
of stinky orange pumpkin parp-gas, and
immediately sprouted arms, legs and a horrid
face. It was now a sting onion! An onion that

could make anyone cry!

'It's alive! Or, at
least, it's undead,'
gasped Rubi.

'**OMG!**' said,
Dennis. 'They've
worked out how to

make more of themselves! Before long, we'll be overrun by undead onions!'

General Parsnip was grumpily pushing a wonky Widl trolley towards the pumpkin king. It squeaked pathetically under a cargo of fresh vegetables . . . that was about to turn eternally rotten.

'Never mind onions making you cry,' warned Dennis, 'Have you ever been poked in the eye by a parsnip?'

'More zombie veg incoming,' said Minnie.

'Pulseless pulses!' whispered Rubi.

'Zombie zucchini,' groaned Stevie.

'A what?' demanded Minnie.

'That's what they call courgettes in America,' explained Stevie.

'Well, in Beanotown we call them . . .

THE ENEMY!'

Rubi couldn't believe what she was seeing. The pumpkin king was able to grow his army, one fart at a time. He wasn't going to settle for five a day either. Beanotown had lost the vegetable plot!

'There's only one person who can dig us out of this,' admitted Minnie. 'It's Dennis time.'

Even wise old Gnasher was surprised. He'd never heard Minnie say *that* before.

SURELY SOME MISTAKE?

Has she had a bump on the head?

Chapter Thirteen

THE VEGETABLE PLOT THICKENS

They filled Minnie in on everything that had happened.

'Beanotown's greatest living writer I.P. Daley says when all seems lost, the plot always thickens. What's the thickest plot in Beanotown?' she asked, already knowing the answer.

Dennis looked blank. His numskulls weren't helping him out here!

'I know!' said Rubi. 'Dennis's plot is completely overgrown with weeds because he neglected it for so long!'

'And what else is there?' said Minnie, tapping a foot impatiently, as if willing a giant earthworm up from the depths. She was waiting for Dennis's brain to catch up with her smart thinking.

'Nope,' said Dennis. 'Not getting it.'

'Some teeny-tiny creatures, maybe?' said
Minnie. 'Who would be awesome at fighting
evil veg if only we had some way of making
them grow big enough?'

'**WHOA!** How could I have forgotten?' said
Dennis. 'The bugs in the insect hotel! If we
dose them with the prof's serums they might
level up! They ate all my veg seedlings when
I planted them. So why wouldn't supersized
bugs eat the supersize zombie veg?'

'Correctomundo, cuz,' replied Minnie,
smirking slightly.

'As a last resort, it could work,' said Rubi.

'You bet, Rubes, your dad's a genius!'
said Dennis, rubbing his hands together in
anticipation, before he messily drenched the
bug hotel with the remaining secret serum . . .

'No, wait!' yelled Vito. 'You've just described an experiment to create, giant . . .

Whoops! Too late. Flash! Bang! Earthquake!

. . . *KILLER BUGS!'*

The humble bug hotel started to throb. As the noise got louder, the hotel swelled up, then burst like a piñata, a battalion of huge superbugs unleashed, and they were ready for lunch.

The gang backed off, terrified, as the bugs zoomed towards them. There was a wasp with a sting the size of a sword! An angry-looking ladybird as big as car! A dragonfly, the same size as a . . . DRAGON! They were doomed!

But all they felt was a
rush of wind that blew
them into the weeds as
the bugs buzzed past them
and headed towards their
veggie buffet.

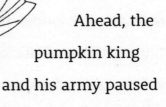

Ahead, the
pumpkin king
and his army paused
and turned towards the
buzzing sounds. They froze with fear, before

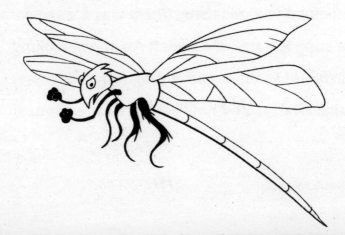

vainly making a run for it. But the bugs started to swoop, and then it was crunch time.

The kids looked away. Except for Minnie. 'Stevie, are you filming this?'

'I'm filming.' *But I'm not sure my gran will let me watch it*, thought Stevie, as carrot juice glooped down onto his lens.

Gnasher was bravely chasing a colossal caterpillar. Any type of cat bugged *him*!

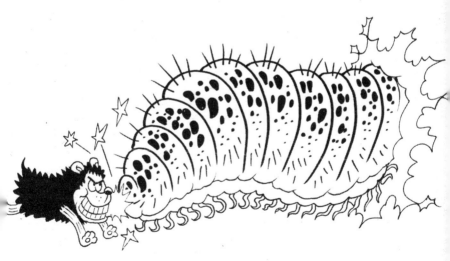

Dennis told the gang to hurry, 'Guys, we'd better get a head start before that giant centipede gets its trainers on!'

Chapter Fourteen

GIVE PEAS A CHANCE!

'It's over,' cheered Dennis. 'The veggies have finally vamoosed!'

'Not all of them,' replied Vito.

'Huh? What?'

'Optimus Pumpkin – the pumpkin king – the insects haven't touched him!'

'That figures. Have you ever tasted pumpkin soup, Vito? Yeuch!'

The ultimate evil vegetable hadn't moved an inch. Around him was a pile of dazed and confused creepy-crawlies surrounded by a toxic cloud of bright-orange gas. The pumpkin king was also the pumpin'-king! His gross gas had protected him from the attack. He was ready to strike again and rebuild his army!

'Keep it down, Dennis! He might hear us,' warned Rubi. Before she could continue, Dennis interrupted loudly.

'Oi, Pumpy-bum. You look like a seedy character. Empty headed!' Optimus Pumpkin slowly turned his head – without his legs moving at all. CREEPY!

'Dennis! cried Rubi. Are you crazy? We've used up all my dad's scientific tips. We've tried boiling and bugging, but Optimus Pumpkin is still here and he could create an entire army before he starts to rot. He's invincible. He's the new mayor. In fact, Beanotown's worst night-mayor and . . .' She could hardly get the last words out, she was so frustrated, '. . . you've just called him PUMPY-BUM!'

She turned to see Dennis beaming with pride. His smile was suddenly cast into eerie shadow. Rubi barely dared to look up.

'WHAT DID YOU CALL ME?'

boomed an angry Optimus Pumpkin. He was way bigger and even scarier than a cyborg teacher intent on squishing every last gram of fun out of school.

> Such as Mr Fayle, who was defeated by our heroes in *The Battle for Bash Street School*, available in all good book shops, and maybe some that aren't so good – The Ed.

Stevie Starr was shivering with fear. He was the tallest of the gang and the pumpkin had squared up to him. It was head-to-head. Or head-to-pumpkin?

The putrid pumpkin ROARED, coating him with wet, sticky seeds. It was like a scene from a horror movie. So scary that even Stevie was too frightened to think about filming.

Rubi looked at Dennis. He winked back at her. He was concentrating . . . hard. It looked like he was constipated. This wasn't the time for bodily functions – or was it?

Dennis was trying to send a thought balloon to Gnasher to let his best mate know it was fine to do what he'd wanted to do from the very beginning of the story. Dennis needed Gnasher to know what he was thinking, so he motioned with his eyes to one vegetable. A massive pea!

All Rubi witnessed was Gnasher sneaking up, right beside the evil pumpkin, and slowly

starting to lift
his hind leg . . .
he wouldn't,
would he?

. . . Peeeeeee!

Optimus
didn't spot the
dog. He was too busy enjoying himself scaring
Stevie! He roared, 'The time has come for
veggies to rule. The time has come for us to
feast on **You**, the way you have gorged upon
us . . .'

Stevie was stuttering with fear. 'I'm a v . . .
veg . . . vegetarian . . .'

'Exactly! You are what you eat. I
believe in a strict vegetarian diet. So, from
this moment on . . . **I ONLY EAT
VEGETARIANS!**'

Stevie closed his eyes and braced himself for the end. At least there would always be his films. The rest of the gang screamed as . . .

Stevie heard a weird fizzing sound and he could smell wee. OH NO! He hadn't? Just as well no one was filming. But, when he dared unscrew one eye, he glimpsed the top of

Optimus Pumpkin's head gently passing his face, descending like an elevator. Whatever was happening?

The pumpkin king was dissolving, that's what! He was turning to mush before Stevie's eyes. Within seconds, all that remained was a luminous yellow pool, with an island of pumpkin seeds and a sorry-looking crown for a lighthouse. The pumpkin had become a squash.

'Result, Gnasher!' proclaimed Dennis. He strode over and ruffled his hero's wiry head. He then pointed to what was left of their foe and said, 'That's what I.P. Daley would call *pulp* fiction!'

He turned to Rubi, in order to explain his pure genius.

'We did all the things your dad told us to do to stop the veggies! The only thing we hadn't tried on them was the thing he'd warned Gnasher NOT to do. Water the veggies the natural way. Instead of peace, we gave pee a chance! I got the idea when I heard the veggies singing.'

'Er, it was PEAS they were singing about, Dennis,' said Rubi.

'Phew!' said Stevie. 'You got rid of the

supersized evil zombie vegetables, but what about the gigantic killer bugs?'

'I was just thinking that too,' said Rubi.

'We could ask them nicely to leave?' offered Vito, rather unhelpfully.

'Or maybe we could call in the SWAT team?' smirked Minnie.

'Listen to me, I'm on a roll. There's a tiny bit of serum left,' declared Dennis. 'We could grow humungous birds to eat them!'

Rubi pinpointed a flaw in the plan, 'They'd put **ƴoυ** on a roll, Dennis. Then eat you. Beanotown seagulls the size of pterodactyls would peck us to pieces. I'm calling my dad . . .'

Rubi put Professor Von Screwtop on speakerphone.

The gang crowded around to listen. 'The thing about my growth serum is that it doesn't affect the DNA of the thing being grown – it just supercharges its growth. If you plant the seeds from a supersize marrow, the next marrows will be normal. Insects don't live that long. By this time next year, they'll be a distant memory.'

Dennis punched the air. 'Yes! So we haven't destroyed the planet by saving Beanotown!'

'Nope. But we need to find them a new MUCH bigger hotel, preferably miles away, and sharpish,' replied Ruby.

'Remember they saved us,' said Vito.

'They deserve to be treated like royalty.'

The search for Bug-ingham Palace had begun!

QUEEN BEE

Chapter Fifteen

BRING OUT THE BUGS!

It was finally judging day for Blooming Britain. There was a buzz about Beanotown and it wasn't just the hum of giant insects. Due to the evil veg, most of the plots had been stripped bare, so it had come down to a battle between the weeds that Dennis had 'lovingly tended' or the mysterious turnip that had sprouted overnight in Walter's patch. If you looked closely, the plant still had a price sticker from Pee & Queue, Beanotown's local garden centre, on it . . .

'Quite a turn-up for the books, isn't it, **LOSERS?**' smirked Walter as he made an L with his fingers and held it up to the gang. As usual, he'd done it the wrong way around . . .

The judges were the presenters from the gardening TV show, *Lettuce Be Thankful*. Dennis hated it because it was on at six o'clock every Sunday evening, right about the time Mum usually asked him, 'Have you done your homework yet?'

The presenters rolled up in a flashy convertible car that made even Wilbur feel envious.

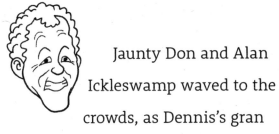

Jaunty Don and Alan Ickleswamp waved to the crowds, as Dennis's gran waited adoringly with her autograph book. Dennis spotted his dad grabbing a selfie with

Heather Gardner and Petunia Rose, the real stars of the show. Their trademark was to always dress to resemble giant flowers. **Petal Power!** Today they looked like giant daffodils, but their perfume helped to cover the stench of rotting vegetables that hung in the air, which was nice.

Mayor Brown smugly welcomed the judges and explained there'd been fewer entries than expected, but they'd be wowed with the fine vegetables on show. He rudely rushed them past Dennis's plot and spread his arms wide as he arrived at Walter's patch.

Jaunty was chewing his lip, clearly confused. 'Why is every vegetable protected by a little canopy and why is everyone in town carrying an umbrella? Are you expecting a sudden downpour?'

'No, sir,' mumbled Walter. His father had kicked him as the question had been asked. He recognised it as a signal to lie in response to every question that followed.

'Then I take it you have lots of rainfall, which makes growing veg easier?'

'Definitely not, sir.'

'Maybe you enjoy extraordinary sunshine to ripen the fruit and veg?' asked Petunia.

'Er, not particularly.'

Heather hollered, 'Then why ever do you all insist upon carrying umbrellas?' She looked annoyed, as if she'd just realised everyone there knew something obvious that she didn't. She hated to look stupid. Which was surprising for someone dressed like a daffodil!

A distant hum drowned out Walter's reply. 'I must apologise, but I think you're about to find out . . . '

Dennis, Rubi, Stevie and Vito threw the judges large umbrellas. They were decorated to look like massive sunflowers. The buzzing became louder. It was a squadron of super bugs, so many that the sky started to darken!

As they flew low overhead, everyone raised their umbrellas. They all had the same design, with a large fly swatter painted on top, apart from those held by the judges, who rushed back to their car, sheltering beneath their giant brollies. The sunflowers on top attracted the bugs, who changed direction and sped after them . . .

'Put the petal to the metal,' yelled Jaunty, as Alan struggled to get the car started wearing his slimy welly boots. But he was going nowhere anyway as Heather was standing, holding the key, reminding him it was her turn to drive. Alan got out of the driver's seat – he knew Heather had a violet streak!

Wilbur rushed over and pleaded with them to stay, stopping them from leaving. This wasn't the type of outcome that would win him *Mayor of the Year!* 'Please don't go! The bugs aren't my fault! What about the prize?'

'Here! Take it! Just get out of our way!'

Jaunty threw the trophy out of the limo and it landed upside down on Walter's head. Petunia blew Wilbur a sloppy kiss as they screeched off. They sped out of town, the

swarm of giant insects following them back to the city. Dennis grinned. Job done.

Wilbur plucked the trophy from Watler's head and held it up triumphantly.

'Hurrah! At last, this stupid town has won a prize! Just a pity the TV cameras aren't here to capture my moment of triumph.'

Dennis burped loudly to get everyone's attention. 'Erm, the judges never actually picked a winner and anyway, what about the CASH prize you promised?'

Wilbur gulped loudly, as if he were attempting to swallow a large potato. 'Ah yes. A very good show put up by everyone, but the first prize can't go to anyone other than Walter, for his terrific turnip.'

Walter proudly held up the pathetic piece

of produce to a distinctly
unimpressed audience.

'BOOOO!'

'FIX!'

'It's twisted, pathetic
and smells.'

'Shut up!' said Wilbur,
'My son is all of those things, but
his turnip is a champion.' He held out the wad
of cash to Walter. Walter smiled uncertainly, as
if he was holding a water balloon timed to burst
any second. It looked as if cheating had paid off.

Wilbur rudely snatched the wad back.
'Children and green should never be seen,' he
muttered, still bitter about how Walter had
successfully outsmarted him during recent
pocket money negotiations.

He started to count the money, fanning it out extravagantly. It looked like a magical money bush. He didn't notice the pathetic turnip split open and a jumbo insect emerge, growing larger and larger as it hovered above a cowering Walter.

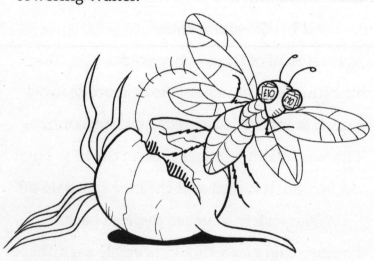

The crowd gasped as one. But there was no danger as the hungry turnip fly had its bug eyes focussed on one thing . . . well,

ten thousand things! It swooped down and
snatched up the prize money, then flew off
with half of it, leaving the rest to flutter slowly
to the ground.

'Scramble!' shouted Dennis, as his
mates joined him in a mad rush to capture as
many falling notes as possible.

Walter and Wilbur were gobsmacked. That
money was reserved for paying someone to
clean their house and build a helicopter wash!

'Catch that cash,' wailed Wilbur. The Browns ran off, chasing the disappearing bug. The mayor lost a shoe in the sticky mud as he jumped to try to catch the bug-lar!

The kids laughed. So did the grown-ups. Wilbur was the least popular mayor in history.

'Did you get any of that on your phone, Stevie?' asked Dennis hopefully.

'Every second! The TV cameras were here after all, Mr Mayor!' Stevie shouted after the disappearing politician.

'What now?' asked Vito.

'Let's go to the den,' suggested Rubi.

'I'll catch you there in ten minutes,' said Dennis, proudly clutching a large banknote. 'I want to buy some more seeds with this unexpected windfall.'

Minnie looked at Vito. Pie Face looked at Stevie. Then they all looked at Dennis.

'OH NO, YOU DON'T!'

Back at the Top Secret Research Station, Professor Von Screwtop was tidying up. He felt a little guilty that he'd nearly ended humanity after Dennis experimented with his secret potions. It was time to get rid of the three remaining jars of secret serum he'd stashed away in his bottom drawer.

He hummed contentedly as he poured them carefully down his sink.

The complex liquids mixed as they disappeared down the plughole and flowed into the ancient maze of pipes that lay deep beneath the Top Secret Research Station . . .

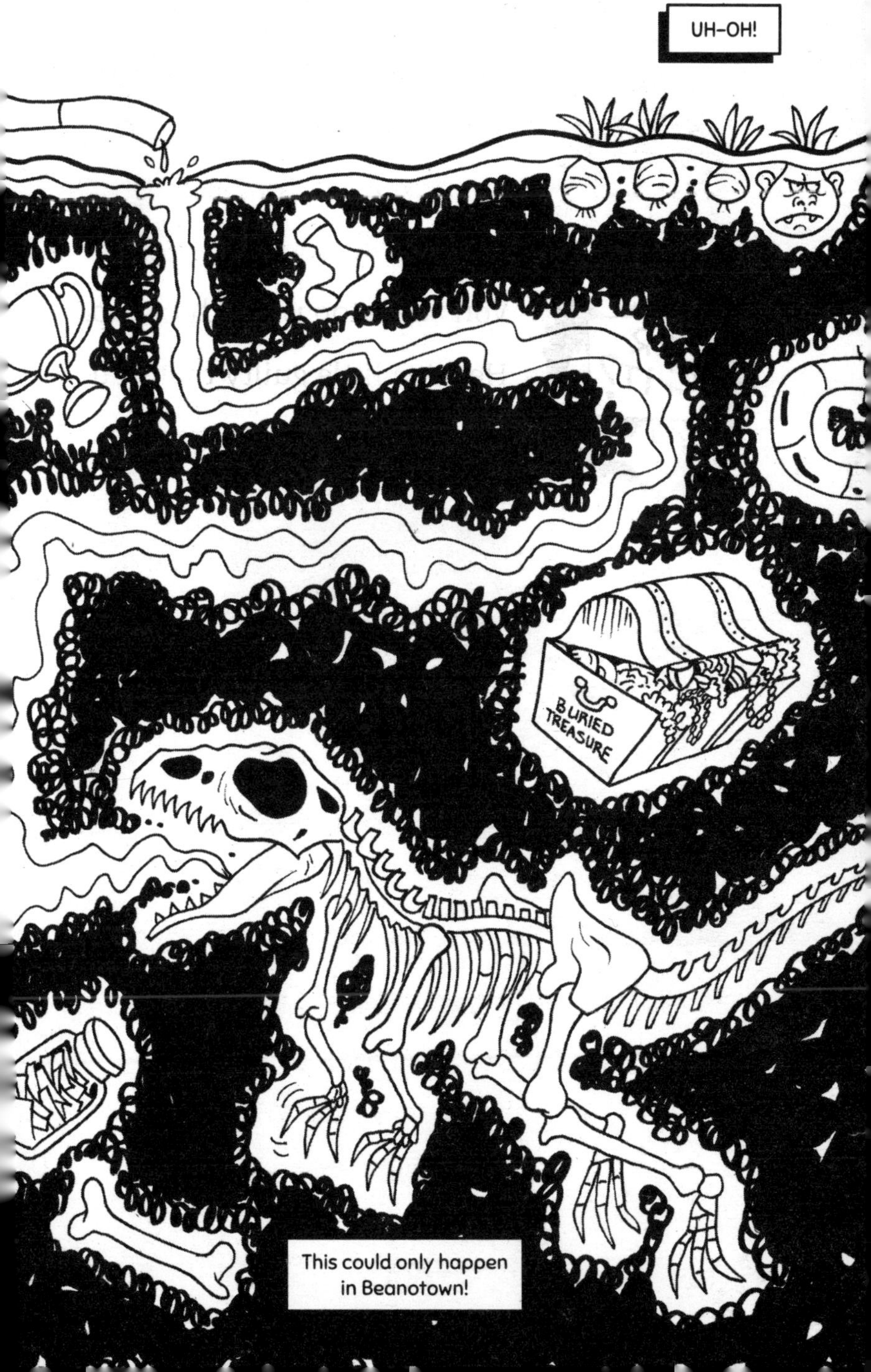
UH-OH!
BURIED TREASURE
This could only happen in Beanotown!

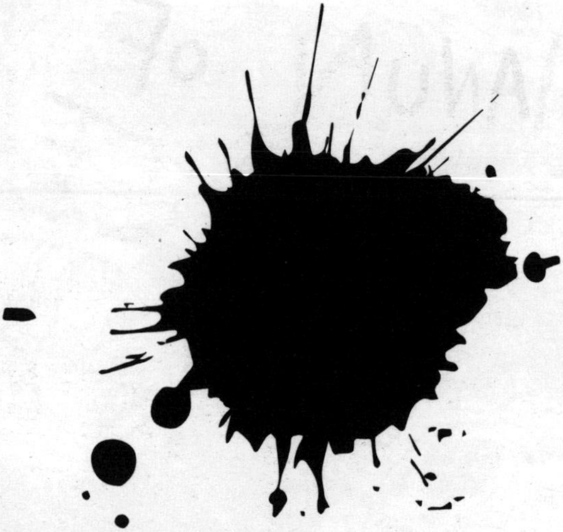

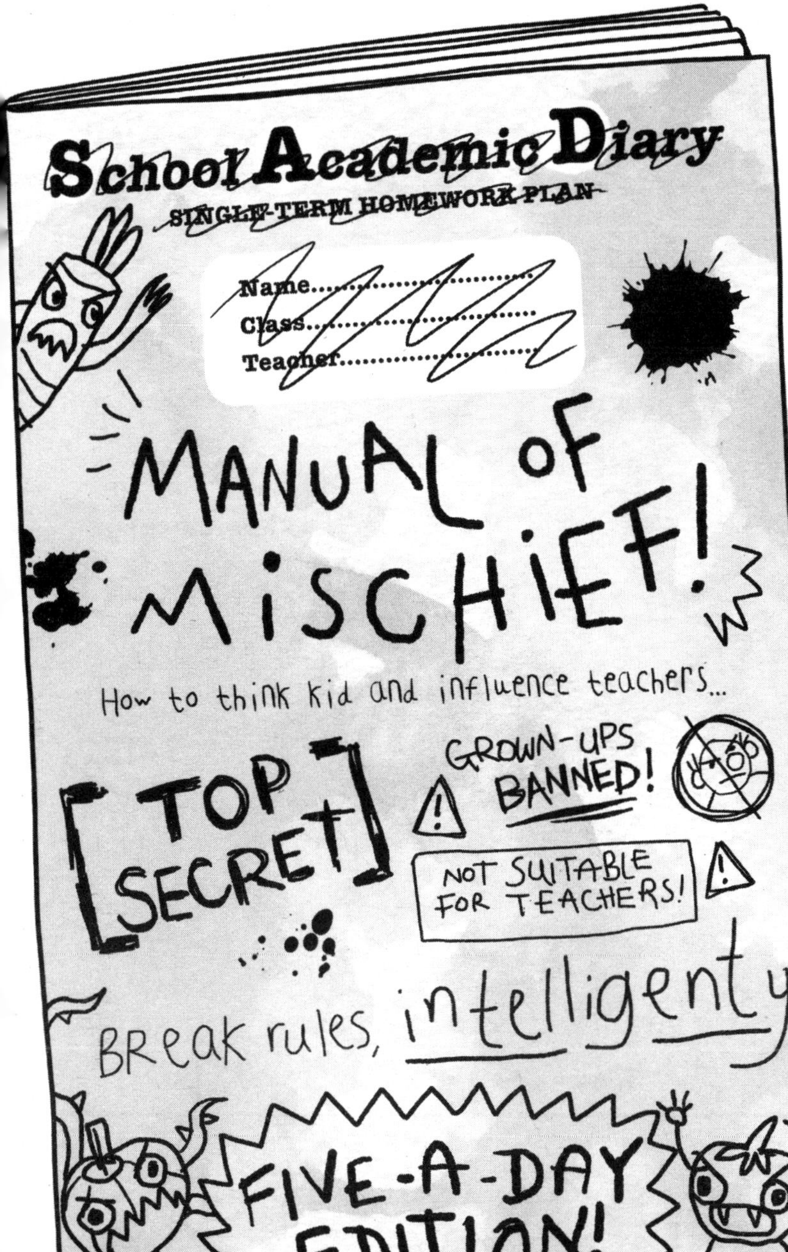

School Academic Diary
SINGLE-TERM HOMEWORK PLAN
Name.......
Class.......
Teacher.......
MANUAL OF MISCHIEF!
How to think kid and influence teachers...
TOP SECRET
GROWN-UPS BANNED!
NOT SUITABLE FOR TEACHERS!
Break rules, intelligenty
FIVE-A-DAY EDITION!

MORE MEGA* MANUAL OF MISCHIEF!!

Every time I.P. Daley writes a book, she let's me stash some cool stuff at the end, as a reward for YOU checking-out every single page!

I've invented all the jokes, pranks and tricks to be

'100% MENACE-GUARANTEED!'

to help YOU (and your mates) win at being a kid.

Unlike Prof Von Screwtop's secret serums, these are tried and tested, by me, Gnasher, Rubes, Stevie, and Vito!

seal of approval →

love it!

REMEMBER, the secret is to never grow-up. It's a **trap!!**

Just look what happened to those Veggies!

Dennis

+ GNASHER →

TOP of the CROPS!

TOP 5 VEGGIE JOKES!

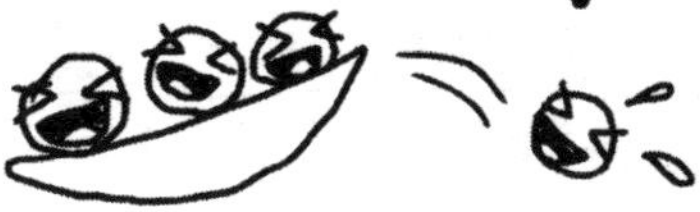

5. What veggie is small, red and whispers?

A hoarse radish!

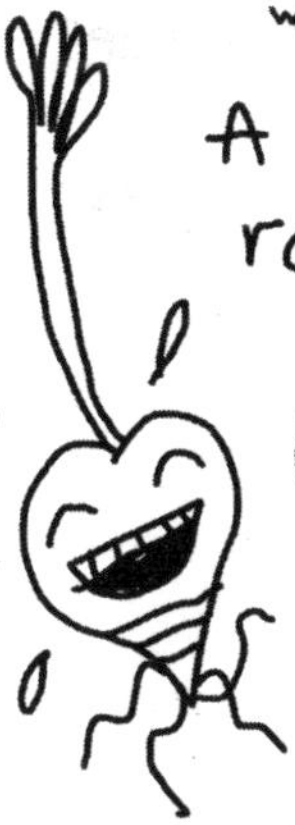

4. What's the fastest vegetable?

A runner bean!

3. What's green and good at tying knots?

Brussel scouts!

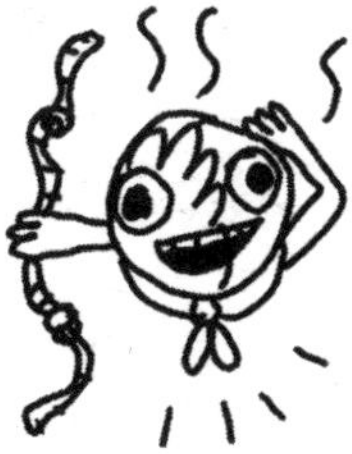

2. How can you tell when they're serving salad for school dinners?

You can't smell burning!

1. What do you get if you cross veggies with a necklace?

A food chain!

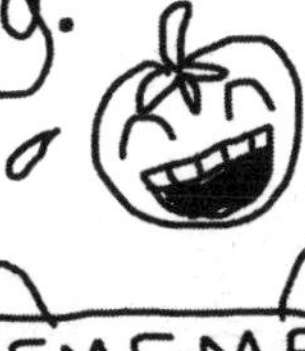

ALWAYS REMEMBER YOUR 5-A-DAY! – That's LAUGHS as well as veggies!

[THE SECRET 7 VEGGIE PATCH!]

Fun facts to flummox friends!

1. Tomatoes aren't veggies! They're fruits (technically, berries). But, in the USA, they are legally vegetables after the Supreme Court passed a rule declaring this!

What am I?!

2. 50% of folks have a gene that allows them to enjoy the taste of Brussels sprouts! That's because they can't taste the bitter flavours in sprouts... the other 50% still find them icky!

Zzz

3. The story that eating carrots helps super-power your vision is

FAKE NEWS!

During the war, Britain had developed new radar tech to help pilots locate their targets in the dark. They didn't want the enemy to suss this, so instead leaked stories that pilots were being fed loads of carrots to improve night vision. The story stuck ...until NOW!

4. A cucumber works as an eraser if you make a mistake writing in ink! Try it!

NOM NOM

NOM

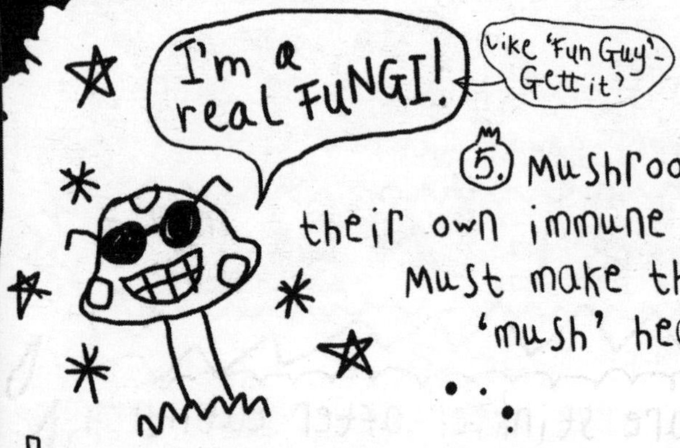
I'm a real FUNGI!
Like 'Fun Guy'- Get it?

5. Mushrooms have their own immune system! Must make them feel 'mush' healthier!

6. Potatoes were the first food to be grown in space.

Definitely **NOT** a Couch-Potato!!

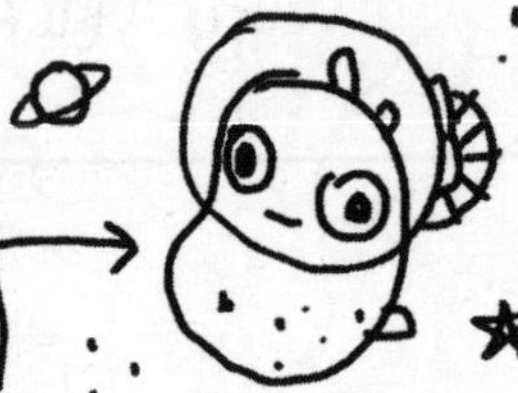

7. There is an orchestra in Austria (Prof Von Screwtop's home country) that uses instruments made entirely from vegetables. After each show they use them to make soup... sounds healthy to us!

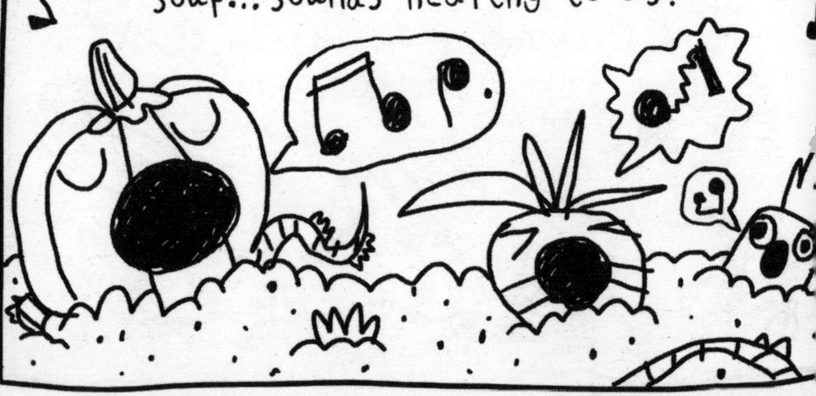

FOR CRYING OUT LOUD!

Farts are stinkier after eating onions! That's because they contain stinky stuff called Sulphur.

It's the sulphur in onions that causes the tears when you slice them. Sulphur, so rude!

It was part of natural evolution, to stop animals eating them...

TOP TIP: If you hold a slice of bread in your mouth when chopping onions it absorbs the sulphur and stops you crying!

KNOW YOUR ONIONS!

ANY QUESTIONS, CLASS?!

Teachers always ask if you have

'Any Questions?'

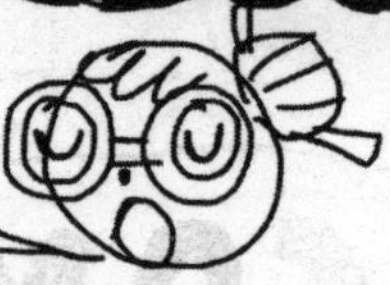

Sometimes it's so they can show off how brainy they are.

Well, if you have THAT type of teacher, ask them ...

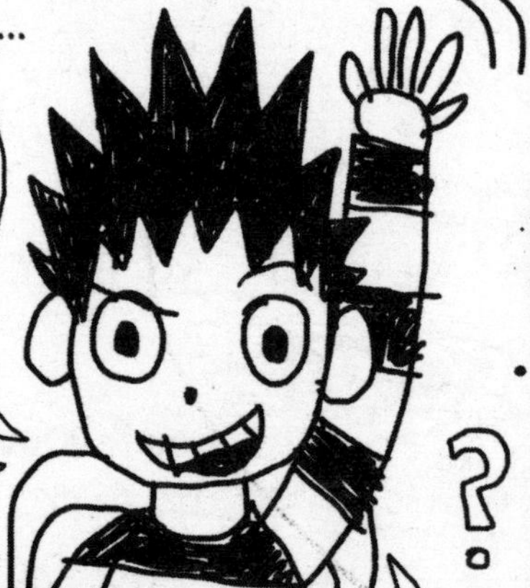

Please may I have some of your sweets?

If dogs have such a good sense of smell, why do they sniff each other's backsides?!

"~~Why are you so~~ boring?

HIGH RISK ALERT!

DENNIS TAKES NO RESPONSIBILITY FOR AN ANGRY TEACHER!

Second Thoughts: WAY TOO CHEEKY!!

The ART of the SUPER-SWIFT COMEBACK!

Sometimes, it isn't troublesome teachers who are the problem. If a pesky pupil or one of your pals gets cheeky, bat it straight back to them with these handy one-liners and a smile!

Oooh!

I know **YOU** are, but what am I?!

Same to you... but times two!

zing!

Yeah! So what if I am?

burn!

THE Riddle of the DEADLY DETENTION!

I'M A PUPIL...

GET ME OUT OF HERE!!

A Bash Street pupil was condemned to the **ULTIMATE LUNCHTIME DETENTION!**

They have to choose between three classrooms to spend it in...

CLASSROOM 1A

Home to stinging scorpions

Small, but ouchy!

CLASSROOM 2A

Home to a Boa Constrictor snake, just dying to give anyone a cuddle...

CLASSROOM 3A

Home to three ferocious lions, who haven't been fed for almost two years!

ROAR

Which would (you) choose if you were the unlucky victim ... I mean, pupil?

ANSWER

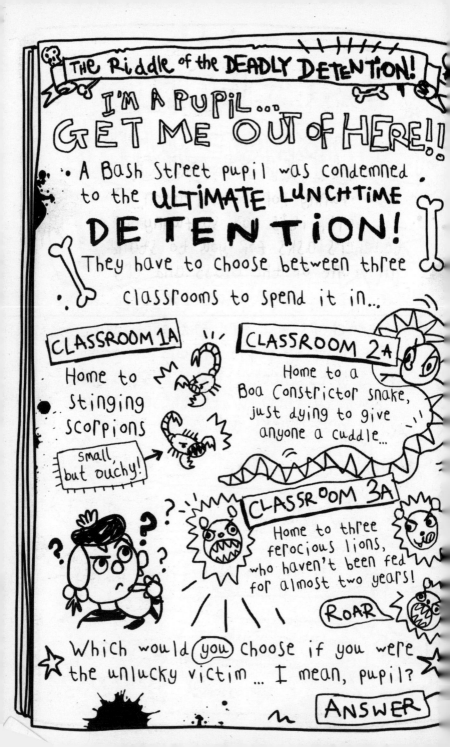

✱ MAGIC ✱ SPELLING

A lot of kids find the word **diarrhoea** funny for some reason...

well, it's not so funny if teachers asks for you to stand up in front of the class and try to spell it!

Unless you have remembered the following secret story:

SPELL it NOT SMELL it!!

Dash **in a real rush hurry Or else accidents!**

If you take the <u>first letter</u> of each word then you have **DIARRHOEA!**

Argh! Quick, to the bathroom!

Classroom 3A. The pool lions are now scattered ponds after having been locked away without food for two years.

Who is I.P. Daley?

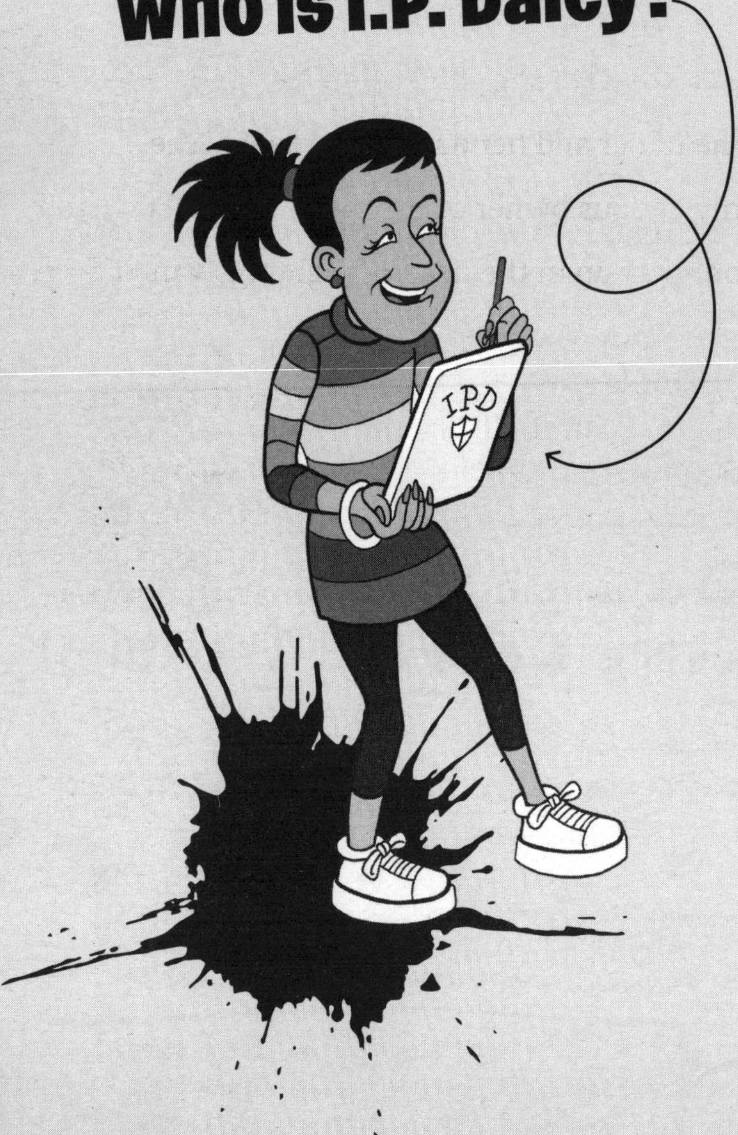
IPD

Ivana Paige Daley was born in Transylvania, a famous region of Romania. She grew up in a spooky old castle, where her mum was the butler and her dad the gardener. The mysterious owner of the castle slept all day and only got up in the dead of night, so Ivana never met Uncle Vamp.

Her favourite rooms in the castle were the greenhouse, where she helped her dad grow his award-winning carnivorous plants; and the library, which was stuffed with adventure books and comics from all round the world. Ivana read them all, which is why she can now speak 18 different languages and sort any bookshelf into alphabetical order in under 12 minutes.

I.P. graduated from Uni, after studying Gelotology – the science of laughter.

During a research trip to the funniest town in the world, she was offered a job at the Beanotown Gazette. Every day she reported the news, but it wasn't funny enough for her . . .

And then Beanotown's resident Yeti librarian introduced her to Dennis and his friends at Bash Street School!

Their mischief was hilarious. Contagious. Outrageous. Ivana cried . . . with laughter.

She had a brainwave. Brainwaves from really smart people can be **MASSIVE!** She'd ask Nigel Parkinson, the Beano comic artist, to draw some funny pictures, and she'd add extra-funny words. Loads of them!

She trawled the Beano archive for the funniest stories in Beanotown's history for inspiration. In amongst the cobwebs, she also

discovered Craig and Mike, two former Beano comic Editors, who help her complete her masterpieces.

Away from writing, her hobbies include collecting joke books, street magic, and looking after her pet bat, Grip, and her collection of giant carnivorous plants. What exactly she feeds them, we don't know . . .

Ivanna chews bubblegum while she writes and is proud to confirm that this is a '60 thousand bubble book.'

Her ambition is to make eight billion people laugh.

P.S. There's one thing Ivana doesn't chuckle at – people laughing at her name . . . **EEK!**

About the Authors

Craig Graham and Mike Stirling were both born in Kirkcaldy, Fife, in the same vintage year when Dennis first became the cover star of Beano. Ever since, they've been training to become the Brains Behind Beano Books (which is mostly making cool stuff for kids from words and funny pictures). They've both been Beano Editors, but now Craig is Managing Editor and Mike is Editorial Director (ooh, fancy!) at Beano Studios. In the evenings they work for I.P. Daley at her Boomix factory, where Craig fetches coffee and doughnuts, and Mike hoses down her personal bathroom once an hour (at least). It's the ultimate Beano mission!

Craig lives in Fife with his wife Laura and amazing kids Daisy and Jude. He studied English so this book is smarter than it looks (just like him). Craig is partially sighted, so he bumps into things quite a lot. He couldn't be happier, although fewer bruises would be a bonus.

Mike is an International Ambassador for Dundee (where Beano started!) and he lives in Carnoustie, famous for its legendary golf course. Mike has only ever played crazy golf. At home, Mike and his wife Sam relax by untangling the hair of their adorable kids, Jessie and Elliott.

READ BRAND-NEW ADVENTURES FROM BEANOTOWN

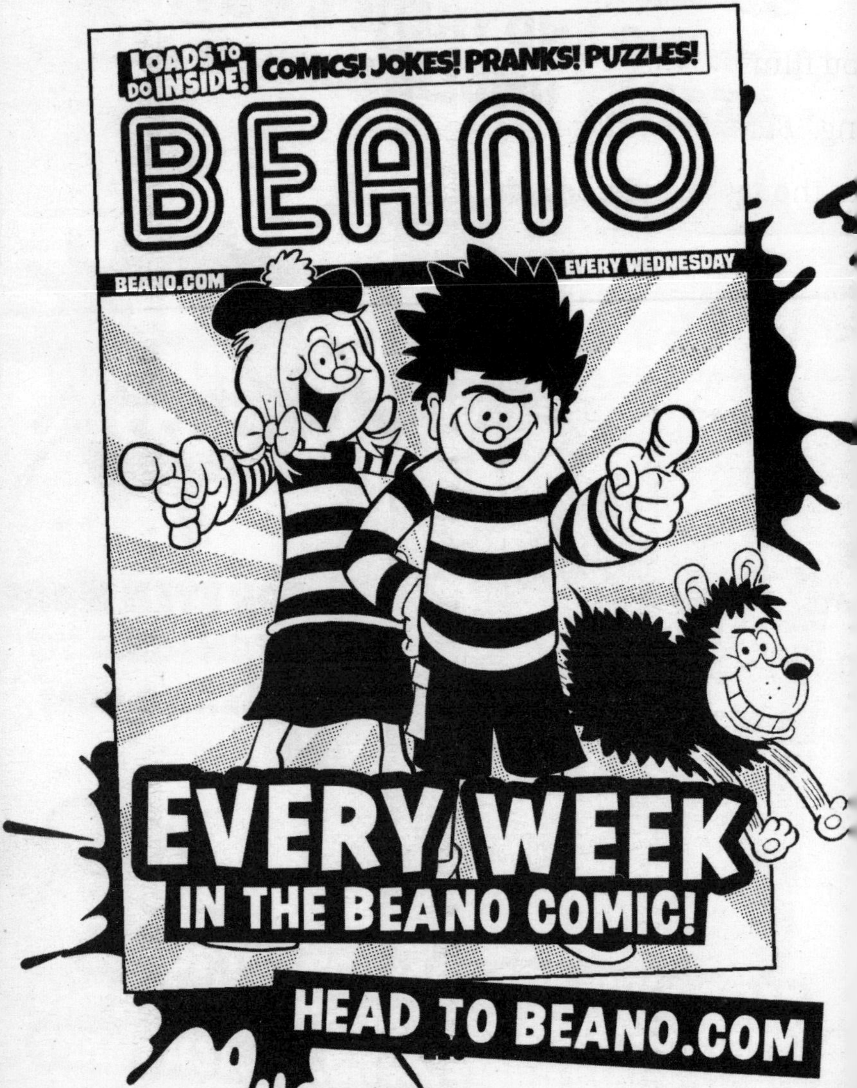
LOADS TO DO INSIDE!
COMICS! JOKES! PRANKS! PUZZLES!
BEANO
BEANO.COM
EVERY WEDNESDAY
EVERY WEEK
IN THE BEANO COMIC!

HEAD TO BEANO.COM